masters of modern
Hebrew literature

M. Z. Feierberg

Whither?
and other stories

translated from the Hebrew
and with an introduction by
HILLEL HALKIN

Philadelphia 5733/1973
The Jewish Publication Society of America

English translation © 1972
By The Jewish Publication Society of America
All rights reserved
Originally published in Hebrew
by Hevrat ha-Sefer (Warsaw, 1904)

ISBN 0–8276–0014–3
Library of Congress catalog card number 72–14057
Manufactured in the United States of America
Designed by Adrianne Onderdonk Dudden

The translation of this book into English was
made possible through a grant from the Adolf Amram Fund

Contents

Whither?
and other stories

Introduction

1

An early, tubercular death was the fate of more than one modern European literary talent, and more than once we see the same sudden maturation in the face of it, the accelerated race against time in which the self of the author strove to be born before the doomed body succumbed. It can be said of Feierberg, too, that death ripened before it reaped. It is hardly the quantity of work in this slim volume that seems most imposing today, though when one considers the conditions under which it was produced, within a space of barely two years, it is not unimpressive either. It is in a sense not even the work itself, which includes several of the finest Hebrew short stories and perhaps the most accomplished Hebrew novella of its time. It is rather the sheer pace of its development, the resolute growth of artistic and psychological mastery that can be traced practically by the month from Feierberg's first published pieces— stories not lacking in promise, to be sure, yet crude attempts nonetheless for an ambitious young man of twenty-two—to the crowning achievement of "Whither?," completed shortly before his death. There is no wavering here, no treading the same ground twice. Each of the handful of stories that he wrote was both a conscious advance on what came before and a step toward something still higher. Herein lies the drama—and triumph—of his brief career.

He was born in September 1874, the second child and only boy in his family, in the provincial town of Novograd-Volinsk in the northwestern Ukraine. His mother tended a small grocery store. His father, Shimon Feierberg, was a ritual slaughterer by trade, a Jew known for his extreme piety at a time and place where a rigidly observed Orthodoxy was itself still a rarely challenged social norm. An adherent of the Hasidic sect of Habad, a movement that combined mystical fervor and an extravagant cabalistic theosophy with a sober commitment to study of the Law, he proudly traced his lineage back to the Jewish aristocracy of the Spanish exile, and in more recent times, to several distinguished martyrs of the faith in Poland and the Ukraine. He was a forbidding, taciturn man, given to fits of temper and tenderness in turn, of which the former grew more common as his son Mordecai Ze'ev, whom he had expected to follow in his footsteps, was drawn to "heretical" thoughts and, worse yet, to the sinful occupation of a writer of fiction in Hebrew, a desecrator, as it were, of the holy tongue. Despite their increasingly strained relations, however, which bordered at times on outright violence, a bond of recognition prevailed between them to the end, at least to judge by the measure of sympathy and respect which Shimon Feierberg is accorded in his son's work.

When Feierberg was still a small boy, the family moved to Hilsk, a small village near Novograd-Volinsk. The interlude there was a pleasant one for him; near the house where he lived were a woods and small stream such as those described in the opening of "Whither?" and the deep feeling for nature that runs through his work was first awakened in these years. In 1884 the family returned for good to Novograd-Volinsk. This was a typical shtetl, to use the Yiddish term for the rural towns and villages of Eastern Europe, in which toward the end of the last century the great majority of the three million Jewish inhabitants of the czarist empire still lived in near-medieval conditions by the tenets of an otherworldly faith. Its 3,000 Jewish families, as Feierberg was caustically to write in later years, maintained "thirty synagogues, four rabbis, and two ritual baths," and comprised

> some eight hundred shopkeepers and their shops, several hundred skilled workers of questionable skill who can never find an honest day's work in town or out

and live off one another's flesh instead, and several hundred more beadles, errand-runners, teachers, and tutors (one-quarter of whom would suffice if our educational system were sensibly reformed), to say nothing of the preachers, the hypocrites, the matchmakers, the go-betweens, the scribes, and all the other common weeds that spring up all over in our untended Jewish fields.[1]

It has become common today to make much of the spirituality and communal solidarity of shtetl life, two qualities that it undoubtedly possessed. Yet nearly all contemporary accounts of it agree that it was a place of grinding poverty and abjectness for the bulk of its inhabitants, who by the middle 1880s were beginning to leave it in droves, whether to emigrate abroad or to take up residence in the larger industrial centers of Russia. Economically pressed to the wall by the obsolescence of the preindustrial trades and services in which it had specialized, its traditional ways and beliefs progressively encroached on by the modern world, the Jewish community of the shtetl was already a society in crisis in Feierberg's childhood, the tragic disintegration of which furnished the subject matter for most of the Hebrew literature of the age. To this his own work was to prove no exception.

In Hilsk he had studied religious subjects with his father, but now he was enrolled in the local heder, the traditional schoolroom of East European Jewry, a lugubrious description of which can be found in his story "In the Evening." He did not excel in his formal studies and preferred instead to dwell in a fantasy

world of his own making. His friend Shmuel Tsvi
Setzer, who composed a biographical memoir of him
after his death, relates:

> His soul was poetic by nature, a tendency which had
> been strengthened in him by several years of village
> life, and he found his talmudic studies arid and lacking
> in nourishment for his sweep of mind and dreamlike
> spirit. . . . His imaginative faculties, on the other hand,
> were strongly developed from childhood on. In the
> days before his death he often told me about the
> flights of fancy he indulged in during this time of his
> life. He would go about for weeks, he told me, lost in
> the reverie that he was cruising on the wings of the
> wind; and more than once, while sitting somewhere
> by himself, or strolling out-of-doors, it would seem to
> him that he was being accompanied by angels or
> devils, with whom he conversed on his way. Or again,
> he would see the heroes of our people, whom our
> Hebrew legend has adorned with thousands of fanci-
> ful tales, rise before him as though from the grave,
> and he would talk and argue with them and follow
> them everywhere. Among his visions were the giving
> of the Torah on Mount Sinai, Elijah [and the priests of
> the Baal] on Mount Carmel, Samuel secretly anoint-
> ing Saul [first king over Israel], the Spanish exiles led
> by [Prince Don Isaac] Abrabanel, and many other
> dramatic scenes which I no longer remember.[2]

After his bar mitzvah he attended the study
house of the Chernobyl Hasidim, the dominant Hasidic sect in town, where the curriculum was mainly
talmudic. Soon, however, he began to read in Hebrew on his own. Slowly his horizons expanded until,
like many another contemporary shtetl adolescent,

he arrived at a painfully earned skepticism regarding the entire system of religious and social values in which he had been raised. This process of self-education he later described in a letter to the Hebrew savant Ahad Ha'am (1856–1927), who, as editor of the Odessa *Hashiloah*, the leading Hebrew literary periodical of its time, was to play a prominent role in his career:

> Our town—Novograd-Volinsk—was a bastion of Hasidism and a stronghold of extreme pietism. My father was a slaughterer there. Naturally, I was educated as per local custom. My imagination was strong and excitable. I hadn't the scantiest notion of the real world, but my curiosity led me from one set of books to another, from the volumes of the Talmud to the writings of the [medieval] moralists, and from the writings of the moralists to the works of the cabalists and philosophers. My head was spinning with world after world, until finally I arrived at the rarified free thought of the Spanish philosophers [i.e., the Aristotelian school of Maimonides and his followers].[3]

From there he proceeded to the literature of the Haskalah, the nineteenth-century secular Hebrew "enlightenment," which served for thousands of young autodidacts like himself as a bridge from the medievalism of the shtetl to a conceptual knowledge of the modern world. Before long he found himself at the head of a small group of like-minded young rebels. The consequences of their association were grave. As told by Shmuel Tsvi Setzer:

> We used to go for long walks outside of town and talk for five or six hours at a stretch, arguing and discussing

at a fever pitch of excitement. Word got about town that a society of heretics had banded together in its midst, and the Orthodox began to harass and molest us. . . . The whole town cursed and hounded us to a man. We were persecuted terribly. They drove us out of the synagogues, burned any of our books that they found, beat us with sticks, and tormented us as best they could. . . . He [Feierberg] was not combative or belligerent by nature, and he suffered unbearably from all this. He was refused meals in his own home, and was humiliated and insulted there all day long.

Worst of all, now that he no longer merited support as a talmudic scholar, he was put to work by his father in the family store to pay for his bed and board, an occupation that proved torturous for his restless spirit. Yet the blow proved a blessing in disguise, for it was during the long hours spent sitting by himself in the empty shop that he first began to write.

He was then about twenty years old and had been engaged for over a year to a girl from a neighboring town, herself a slaughterer's daughter who was several years younger than he. The match was a traditional one, arranged by the young couple's parents, but the two were independently attracted to each other at first sight. They never married, both because of Feierberg's health and the general insecurity of his situation, but they continued to meet and correspond until close to the end of his life, when he reluctantly consented to break off the engagement at the insistence of the girl's parents. Ironically, his fatal illness began with a lingering cold that he contracted while on a visit to his bride's home to draw up the betrothal terms. The condition appeared trivial at first and was allowed to develop untreated until the symptoms of tuberculosis appeared.

In the winter of 1895–96 he traveled to Warsaw for medical consultations. While there he submitted several of his poems and prose fragments to Nachum Sokolov (1859–1936), the influential editor of the Hebrew daily *Hatsefirah*, who in turn showed them to the celebrated Hebrew and Yiddish author I.L. Peretz (1851–1915). The two men advised him to concentrate on fiction, for which they deemed him better suited, and encouraged him in his efforts. The meeting endowed him for the first time with a firm sense of his literary vocation. He spent the summer in the countryside on doctors' instructions and then returned to his native town. Henceforward he was to devote himself steadily to his writing. His first published story, "Yankev the Watchman," appeared in Sokolov's *Hatsefirah* in December 1896, while the others followed over the next two years.

These last years were excruciating ones for him. On the one hand, he was now working at an intense creative pitch that frequently possessed him for days on end. Apart from his stories, he wrote a small amount of literary criticism and reportage in this period, and devoted what time he had left to the organization of Hebrew and Zionist discussion groups in Novograd-Volinsk and several neighboring towns. At the same time, however, his health continued to worsen, and his relationship with his family, especially with his father, deteriorated still further in spite of his illness. Not having the money to rent a room of his own, he frustratedly wrote to Ahad

Ha'am in March 1898, during a hiatus when he was not writing at all: "[I feel that] my talents are not developing properly; I have many creations within me, and my head is swarming with literary material of all kinds, but for lack of a place to work there are times when I scarcely hold a pen in my hand for months on end."

For stretches of time he lived and worked at the houses of friends, only to be constrained to return home in the end, where he was treated with open vindictiveness, as behooved an unpenitent sinner and renegade to the faith. Another friend, Asher Wohl, relates the following incident:

> I cannot pass in silence over an episode that illustrates the conditions under which Feierberg wrote his best works. . . . I was living nearby at the time and once had to go to his house on some business. The scene that met my eyes there pained and revolted me terribly. Feierberg sat leaning by the table on one arm, his eyes staring down at a sheet of paper that lay before him. His face was even paler than usual and his breath came in spurts. His fanatical father was circling around him with a crazed, malicious finality and screaming like a man gone wild: "Ahad Ha'amchik!* Heretic! Death is already upon you! I can see its mark on your face!" . . . I did my best to calm him. Feierberg, however, did not even glance up at me. I realized then that he was suffering less from his father's lunacy and insane speech than from my having been a witness to so frightful a scene. He handed me a

*Although Ahad Ha'am was far from hostile himself to Jewish religious tradition, as a secular intellectual he was anathema to the Orthodox camp nonetheless.

chapter of his essay "On Our Hebrew Literature and Its Obligations,"[4] and I hurried to leave the house.[5]

He spent most of 1898 working on his novella "Whither?," the final corrections of which were completed in February 1899. A few days later he took to bed for the last time. He was attended throughout by Shmuel Tsvi Setzer, who wrote of his death:

> His last illness lasted some thirty-three hours. About two hours before he died he asked me whether the clock [on the wall of his room] was still running, and in fact, it had stopped. It occurred to me that it could have a bad effect on a critically ill man of his imagination to tell him this, and so I pretended that it hadn't. About ten minutes before he passed on he asked again. Again I dissembled. Imagine my astonishment, then, when I later found written in his diary: "There are two patients in this room, my clock and myself, and only our symptoms are different: I suffer lying down and it standing up. I'm sure that on the day that I die it will stop running too."

An unexpectedly large crowd turned out for his funeral. Among the mourners were many of his fellow townsman who only shortly before had joined in abusing him. Few could have read his stories or known of the compassion with which their own lives were treated there; now, however, with a kind of folk-prescience, it was borne in on them at last that a rarer spirit than their own had indeed lived among them. As described by Asher Wohl:

> No sooner had word spread of Feierberg's death than a great crowd began to gather: not only the more

cultured and educated men and women of our town, but many of the Orthodox and Hasidim too, assembled before his house, where they waited to accompany the body to the Great Synagogue. There the town cantor chanted the prayer for his soul; after which the service was performed in several other synagogues as well, and we proceeded [to the cemetery] outside of town. I was born in Novograd-Volinsk and have spent nearly all my life there, yet I have never seen such a great, tumultuous funeral before. A huge throng, hundreds and hundreds of people, followed the bier, and a hundred or more came to the cemetery too, though it was a cold, rainy night and the distance to there from our town was a good four or five versts.

Religious passions pursued him even now. His father, his legal executor, refused permission for his stories to be republished in a volume of their own, claiming that the offense given to God in his son's lifetime should at least be consigned to a charitable oblivion in his death. The deceased's friends and admirers sought to prevail upon him, but in vain; and it was not until 1904 that he finally relented and a thin edition of Feierberg's work was allowed to appear.

2

Feierberg was by temperament part of the romantic reaction to the literature of the Haskalah that took hold among Hebrew writers in Eastern Europe in the late 1880s and 1890s. This reaction assumed different and even mutually hostile forms, but it had in common a rejection of the optimistic rationalism of Haskalah thought, with its faith in scientific progress, political liberalism, and the integration of the Jew into the social and cultural fabric of European bourgeois life. There are, of course, seemingly romantic elements in Haskalah fiction too, as in the biblical novels of Mapu; but here one is dealing with a pastoral mode whose idealized past is as artificial as it is remote. In the real struggle between tradition and modernization that occupies the center of nearly all Haskalah writing, there is little room for doubt as to where the hopes and allegiances of the Haskalah writer lie.

Like all East European Hebrew authors of his generation, Feierberg came to literature through the Haskalah, and its influence on his earliest efforts must have been great. Even "Yankev the Watchman" shows him still largely unweaned from it in both substance and style. The story was written in the autumn of 1896, when he was staying with a friend at a country house near Novograd-Volinsk. Nearby lived an old Jewish tailor who had been impressed into the czarist army as a youth during the reign of Nicholas I,* and it was his reminiscences that Feierberg used as the basis for his tale. The struggle of the poor, simple Jew to preserve his integrity in the face of life's conspiracies against him, the machinations of

---

*The "cantonists," as these unfortunate youngsters were called, were taken by the Russian government from the Jewish community at the age of twelve according to a system of quotas, boarded out for several years in Christian homes, and then drafted into the army for a twenty-five-year term of service. Few of those who survived the ordeal did so as Jews, and wealthier Jewish families inevitably saw to it, whether through bribery or other means, that the victims were taken from among the poor. The practice was discontinued after Nicholas's death in 1855.

the reactionaries and the rich within the Jewish community, "that distant day to come when unscarred human beings will write the history of mankind's awakening"—all echo familiar Haskalah themes. Equally derivative are the didactic tone and high-flown prose of the story: even the descriptions of nature, with their "moon concealed in its heavenly mansion" and "trees that wave their green leaves in applause," bear the unmistakable stripe of Haskalah rhetoric, or *melitsah,* that pastiche of rabbinic and neobiblical diction that served as a standard of elegance in the world of nineteenth-century Hebrew letters. Yet there are other passages in "Yankev the Watchman" in which the authentic voice of the artist can already be heard, such as the account of the winter nights in the young boy's home. Here the prose is unaffected and plain and bears the characteristically hushed cadences of Feierberg's best work to come. One can only conjecture whether "Yankev the Watchman" would seem a better or worse piece today had it not been heavily cut by the editors of *Hatsefirah,* so that, as its author unhappily complained in a letter to Ahad Ha'am, "the figure of the hero now seems undeveloped, though his portrait emerged a perfect whole from my hands."

"The Shadows" was written soon after, in the winter of 1896–97.[6] Though it shares most of "Yankev the Watchman's" stylistic shortcomings, it reveals Feierberg in the unmistakable process of freeing himself from them as well. Still present too is the moralizing tone,but significantly this is no longer directed against the forces of "reaction" but rather against those of "progress," as represented by the

society of "emancipated" Jews whom the narrator
meets at the end. (Such a "social club" had indeed
been opened in Novograd-Volinsk that same winter,
and two letters published by Feierberg in the Hebrew press were highly critical of it.[7])

At the heart of the reevaluation of the conven-
tional Haskalah imagery of future "light" and past
"darkness" in "The Shadows" lay Feierberg's growing conviction—one arrived at despite his own persecution at the hands of the Orthodox of Novograd-
Volinsk—that in calling on East European Jewry to
remodel itself in the image of a liberal, secular
Europe, the Haskalah was asking it to sell its spiritual
birthright for a mess of thin pottage indeed. At the
same time, he did not wish the story to be read as a
revivalist plea for a historically doomed way of life.
Rather, as he wrote to Ahad Ha'am in submitting
"The Shadows" for publication to *Hashiloaḥ*, it was
a question of salvaging what one could from the im-
pending collapse of a tradition:

> In "The Shadows" . . . I was not specifically intending
> to attack "the broader life" of the young generation
> or to glorify that of the old: the new is gradually taking
> hold among us whether literature likes it or not, and
> the old, no matter how holy or exalted it may be, is
> fated to disappear. We could not bring the "devil" [of
> modernity] back to the synagogue even if we sought
> to, but we must bring the synagogue out to the
> "devil." And the most trustworthy medium for this
> purpose, of course, is Hebrew literature. One has to
> be foolish or ignorant to argue that our world [of the
> shtetl] is lacking in outstanding color or material.
> . . . All that is needed is the artist and craftsman who

can plumb the Jewish heart and whatever beats within it. . . . Tremendous spiritual treasures lie buried beneath the ruins of these obscure streets [of the ghetto]. We cannot linger among them, yet neither can we allow them to remain behind. We must find a way to bring them too to "the broader life" outside.

This letter placed Feierberg squarely on Ahad Ha'am's side in the polemical debate that the latter was engaged in with the young Hebrew writer Micah Yosef Berditshevsky (1865–1921). Berditshevsky, who had been influenced by the writings of Nietzsche and had sought to apply their critique of Western culture to the context of European Jewry, was in revolt against the Haskalah as well, but from the opposite pole: the Haskalah, he argued, had been a merely reformist protest that did not go far enough, for only a total repudiation of exilic Jewish history could pave the way for the heroic "new Hebrew" who alone might survive the shipwreck of East European Jewry. The debate over whether Hebrew literature should serve as an instrument of cultural revolution, as proposed by Berditshevsky, or of evolutionary conservatism, as held by Ahad Ha'am, was a seminal one for the modern Hebrew revival, and by extension, for the Zionist movement that grew out of it; yet quite apart from the broader issues involved (on which he sided with Ahad Ha'am in any case, as he later made clear in an "Open Letter to Mr. Berditshevsky," written in 1898[8]), it seemed evident to Feierberg that no Hebrew writer could reject the world of the shtetl as subject matter without cutting off the very limb on which he sat. Ahad Ha'am, however, was not taken with "The Shadows," which he returned to its author with a brief rejection note stating that "I like things to be simple and clear and not full of 'symbols' and fancy phrases."[9] The story was first published in 1898.[10]

"A Spring Night" was written in the spring of 1897,[11] and with it Feierberg's apprenticeship may be said to have come to an end. The prose has become more direct, though still not entirely purged from its rhetorical posture. Gone too are the tendentious opening proem and the editorial end, which is here replaced by a poignantly unresolved tone. As in "The Shadows," the adolescent conflict in "A Spring Night" pits loyalty to the ancestral world of the shtetl against the need to break free of its cloistering walls; yet here the scales have tilted urgently back toward the latter. A more sparingly written story than either "Yankev the Watchman" or "The Shadows," "A Spring Night" is a more desperately vulnerable one too. In the character of the gray-haired narrator mourning his "misspent" life it is not difficult to detect the twenty-three-year-old author who had growing reason to suspect that he himself was living on borrowed time. In early spring of that year, indeed, his condition had worsened; the fatal disease had spread to his throat. From here on the clock had begun to run out.

3

As far back as the prose fragments that he showed to Nachum Sokolov in Warsaw, Feierberg had conceived of a character whom he half-whimsically named *Hofni Ba'al Dimyon,* "Hofni the Fantast."* Hofni was the name given by him to the adolescent narrator of "The Shadows" as well, and in the letter that accompanied the story to Ahad Ha'am he remarked:

> This character of mine, "Hofni the Fantast," is not really a spinner of fantasies, but he is a Jew with a live Jewish heart; a person to whom both his Jewishness and his [general] culture are equally precious and important; who is continually colliding and continually warring with life, for he refuses to compromise whatever he judges sacred in his Jewishness or his ideals, and life, in all its present and corruptible grossness,

*The somewhat unusual biblical name of Hofni was never in actual use among East European Jews, which no doubt made it appropriate for the idiosyncratic character that Feierberg had in mind. Yet the name had a deeper significance for him too, as is clear when one looks at the single passage in the Bible in which it appears. This is in First Samuel, where it belongs to one of hereditary high priest Eli's two sons. There we read of how "the sons of Eli . . . knew not the Lord," so that when "Eli was very old; and he heard all that his sons did unto all Israel . . . he said unto them: 'Why do ye such things? for I hear evil reports concerning you from all this people. Nay, my sons; for it is no good report which I hear the Lord's people do spread abroad. If one man sin against another, God shall judge him; but if a man sin against the Lord, who shall entreat for him?' But they hearkened not unto the voice of their father, because the Lord would slay them." In punishment, the story continues, "And there came a man of God unto Eli, and said unto him: 'Thus saith the Lord. . . . I said indeed that thy house, and the house of thy father, should walk before Me for ever; but now the Lord saith: Be it far from Me: for them that honour Me I will honour, and they that despise me shall be lightly esteemed. Behold, the days come, that I will cut off thine arm, and the arm of thy father's house, that there shall not be an old man in thy house . . . and all the increase of thy house shall die young men.' " Hofni and his brother die soon after in a battle against the Philistines in which the ark of the Lord is lost. When Eli hears of the news he falls from his seat and dies too, the priesthood passing from his now heirless family forever.

refuses to compromise either. . . . Unfortunately, though . . . we see that people like Hofni are really considered mad, which is why I have named him 'the Fantast.' I still have not done with my Hofni, and indeed have great plans for him, if only I can find him a place in our literature.

When he next appeared in "The Calf," however, which was written in early summer of 1897 and published soon after in *Hashiloah*, Hofni was not the adolescent of "The Shadows," much less the complex young Jew of his times described in the letter above, but an innocent boy whose conscious existence had yet to be impinged on by the world beyond the shtetl. Such, in fact, seem to have been the "plans" for him to which Feierberg had referred, for the next time he wrote to Ahad Ha'am he stated: "I am determined to present the complete world of the Jew in these tales, and so I have started from the period of childhood." Hofni, in other words, was to be the autobiographical hero of a series of stories that would take him from boyhood to maturity and trace the gradual awakening of consciousness in a typical son of the shtetl. What was intended, indeed, was nothing less than a psychological anatomy of East European Jewish life, for as Feierberg continued in his letter:

If only it were granted him, the writer of these lines would like to trace the most inward form of our outwardly manifested world. . . . The air the Jew breathes, the sky that he looks at, the earth that he walks upon, and all the outward visions that he beholds each day assume a different form and aspect in his soul than they do in reality or for others. . . . This, in my opinion, is the only answer to the question of how our literature can become a universal one. . . . We do not owe our readers all manner of wondrous adventures, but we do owe them, quite simply, our own inner world, with all its anguish and anger, its joy and elation, which each of life's spectacles evokes in us every moment. We need to show . . . what is suffering and poverty with others and what is suffering and poverty with us; what our public life consists of and what theirs; what the life of the individual, his drives, ambitions and responsibilities, is like in our case and what it is like elsewhere; what we find holy and profane and what others do; what we possess that they don't and what they possess that we don't; how our society has evolved to its present state, and how it has developed those myths, manners, and customs that shape and influence our lives.

Such a project might have appeared grandiose for a writer who had thus far demonstrated so limited a mastery of his craft; but the very fact that he now chose to begin with a child further removed from himself in experience and years than the narrators of "The Shadows" and "A Spring Night" enabled Feierberg to objectify fictionally a character and a situation in a way he had failed to do before. If "The Calf" is his first truly successful story, as well as his first in which the life of the shtetl assumes a tangibility of its own, this is in measure because it is the first to be written from that minimum of distance required for an accurate perspective.

"The Calf" is on the surface a simple story of a boy's moral conflict over the killing of an animal and his inability to reconcile what he sees with his idea of God's justice. Hofni's religious crisis in "The Calf" is no less real than that of the narrator of "The Shadows" or "A Spring Night"; on the contrary, precisely because it is a child's and cannot conceive of moral relatives, it is all the more anguished and direct. At the same time, however, there is another, symbolic aspect to "The Calf" that hints at psychological depths not previously present in Feierberg's work. Readers of the story may be struck by the fact that the calf is to be slaughtered when it is eight days old, the same age at which, Hofni informs us, his baby brother was "killed" by the Angel of Death. In Jewish tradition, of course, the eighth day of life has but one association, which is with the rite of circumcision. Whether or not this allusion, with its distant yet fearful intimations of child sacrifice and biblical myth, was fully conscious on Feierberg's part (the fact that in the story, as opposed to real life, the slaughterer is linked to the mother suggests perhaps that it was not), it clearly represents a motif of great power, one that was to take increasing hold on Feierberg's imagination and that was soon to surface more boldly in the pages of "Whither?"

If the evocations of symbol and myth barely intrude on "The Calf," they are the very stuff out of which "In the Evening," which was written during the autumn of 1897,[12] is woven. Here, one feels, Feierberg is at last in his native imaginative element. Indeed, with its intricate story within a story, its skillful counterpointing of the magical world of folktale and legend with the harsh reality of the cold, wet autumn night in the shtetl, and its flawless command of narrative pace and mood, "In the Evening" is a little masterpiece of its kind. So sure are its conception and execution that it is difficult to believe that it could be the work of the same novice who had written "Yankev the Watchman" barely a year before.

While its complex fictional form was a new departure for Feierberg, however, the thematic content of the story differs less from his previous work than might appear at first glance. Once again the closed, ancestral walls of the shtetl confront a hostile yet alluring world outside. Once again it is neither violence nor persecution that threaten to break the sacred circle, but the "music" of the senses and of the full life that beckons beyond. Once again the young Jew must choose between irreconcilable opposites, one pulling him mightily one way, the other "just as mightily back." And once again, too, as in "The Calf," an even darker ambivalence than this haunts the story. The landowner and his world are creatures of Samael, to be sure, demonic enticements. Yet looking through the eyes of the child, what is one to make of the saintly old father, who appears two times in a dream to his terrified son—magically spirited away from him on the eve of his circumcision!—and threatens to kill him if he is not obeyed? Little wonder that Hofni can only say of his feeling at the end of his mother's tale that "good or evil, holy or unclean . . . it was dreadful." Dread lies at the center of "In the Evening," radiating outward in every direction: dread of the unknown, of course, but of the familiar too, and of what it may prove to conceal.

"The Amulet" was written soon after "In the Evening," in late autumn of 1897, and forms a direct sequel to the latter. The story begins with Hofni's waking in a fright in the middle of the night and ends with his initiation into the knowledge that the dread that he feels is an inescapable part of his life. It is, in fact, the permanent state of the Jew, who is surrounded in this world by divine and demonic forces that struggle for possession of his soul, that may even masquerade as one another, and from which it is impossible to flee. There is, in effect, no way out: he can only accept his condition and follow the path of his forefathers before him by becoming a soldier in a never-ending cosmic war. It is suggestive that whereas the parental presence in "The Calf" and "In the Evening" is provided by Hofni's mother, "The Amulet" begins with her again and then shifts abruptly to his father. It is as if with this transition he has permanently stepped out of the maternally protected world of childhood and into that arena between God and the devil that is the station of every male Jew. In "Whither?" father and son appear alone by themselves. It was here, for Feierberg, that the crucial confrontation lay.

4

Feierberg had planned his Hofni stories to form part of an extended series, yet after finishing "The Amulet" he did not pursue them any further. It is possible that, having so quickly proved adept at the short story, he felt the need to go on to a broader, more novelistic framework; possibly too he had now come to realize that time would not permit him to bring Hofni gradually along to manhood as originally intended. In any case, he broke off the cycle and after several unproductive months, in the spring of 1898, began work on "Whither?," the last and the longest of his tales. He worked steadily on it through the summer and autumn and finished in early winter of the year.

The Nachman of "Whither?" is, of course, none other than Hofni by a different name, but a Hofni more fully developed in character and in time. His father, too, is familiar from "The Amulet," and in the opening pages of the novella the veiled struggle between them comes to its symbolic head: if as an adolescent in the study house Nachman has come to feel that he is being sacrificed like Jephthah's daughter on the altar of an implacable God, his instinctive thought upon committing his act of ritual sacrilege in the synagogue on the Day of Atonement is that "Cain had killed Abel his brother, but he had killed his own father." Yet in the final analysis, the father in "Whither?" emerges not as an insensitive religious tyrant but as a lonely and even heroic figure struggling to defend and transmit an archaic faith on whose banner is emblazoned the biblical verse "And ye shall be holy unto the Lord your God." There are no sentimental concessions to this faith in "Whither?" but there is not the slightest condescension toward it either. Indeed, nowhere else in modern Hebrew fiction can one find so passionate yet impartial an account of the inner world of East European Jewish pietism, that extreme historical culmination of Jewish religious experience, which, if it burdened its faithful with a morbid fear of sin and an obsession with ritual detail on the one hand, paid them the supreme honor on the other of placing them at the very spiritual center of the cosmos and granting them the power to move heaven and earth, to even bring the Messiah, if only they proved equal to the task.

The psychological tensions generated in a child by such a simultaneously ego-repressing and ego-inflating outlook might well become insupportable, and indeed, Nachman does go "mad" in the end, though hardly in a clinical sense. His "madness," rather, is more social than psychological: it is not that he has in any real sense lost his sanity as an individual, but rather that while he is unable to go on functioning within a religious tradition whose premises he can no longer accept, he is unable to function outside it either. As such his situation was clearly intended by Feierberg to represent the dilemma of an entire generation of young East European Jews like himself, who had lost an old world, as Nachman's friend Yehezkel puts it, without gaining a new one in its place. By "killing" his father Nachman has indeed won his freedom, but it is a freedom in some ways more terrible than the bondage of the God he has overthrown.

Though the final pages of "Whither?" seek to point a way out of this dilemma, if not for Nachman then at least for his generation as a whole, it is likely that when Feierberg began the novella he was still uncertain how to end it. (Interestingly, he first tentatively titled the story "The Heretic," which he changed to the more programmatic "Whither?" while the work was in progress.) It was this same impasse of course that led, in Eastern Europe in the

early 1880s, to the first stirrings of Zionism, that most
ambitious of all modern attempts to redefine the
question of Jewish identity in other than traditional
terms, and to the extent that Feierberg offers a solution in "Whither?" it is a Zionist one too. Because the
events of the novella ostensibly take place in the
narrator's childhood—we are told on the first page of
the story that he was still a boy in the heder when he
heard of them—it was chronologically consistent of
Feierberg to refer to Zionism in the final chapter of
"Whither?" as "a new movement abroad in the Jewish world." Yet it is clear that this chapter was written under the impact of contemporary develop-
ments, particularly the activity of Herzl, who had
burst like a meteor on the Jewish scene with the
publication of his *Die Judenstaat* in 1896. It was
above all Herzl's magnetic influence on the Jewish
masses of Eastern Europe that aroused Zionist emotions from the lethargy into which they had sunk in
the course of the 1890s and that was instrumental in
the convening of the historic First Zionist Congress
in Basel in 1897.

Nachman's final oration, however, is hardly a
tribute to Herzl. On the contrary, in it Feierberg was
once again following Ahad Ha'am, who had taken
strong exception to Herzl and his school of "political"
Zionism from the outset. Whereas Zionism, Ahad
Ha'am held, was a response at the deepest level to a
spiritual and historical crisis whose dynamics were
autonomously Jewish, and whose resolution must also
be so, it was for Herzl, he felt, little more than a
logical solution to the problem of Christian anti-
Semitism, the successful implementation of which

was a matter for international diplomacy and high finance—a charter for Palestine to be obtained from the Turkish Porte at such-and-such a price, so many Jews to be transported and settled there at so much per head, etc. After two visits to Palestine in the early 1890s, Ahad Ha'am had already warned against the tendency of Jewish settlers there to play the role of European colons vis-à-vis the Arab natives, and Herzl's eagerness to collaborate with the European imperial powers in order to obtain a homeland for the Jews only strengthened his fears in this direction. This theme too appears in Nachman's speech, yet within a historicophilosophical context that is itself completely alien to the positivist tenor of Ahad Ha-'am's thought.

On what other sources might Feierberg have drawn for Nachman's rather singular theories about the cycles of civilization and his speculations concerning an alternation of dominance between East and West and the role to be played by the Jews in the reascendance of the former? Partly perhaps on such nineteenth-century Hebrew authors as the philosopher Nachman Krochmal (1785–1840), who had been influenced by Hegel, or the Haskalah figure Yehudah Leib Levin (1844–1925), who had already written in the 1880s of a coming renaissance of Asia in which the Jews would take their rightful place; partly too, no doubt, on various strands of fin-de-siècle thought that were circulating throughout Europe in the 1890s. (Apart from the "reading list" attributed to Nachman in the penultimate chapter of "Whither?" Feierberg was reading widely at this time in Russian and German, the two European lan-

guages that he mastered toward the end of his life.)
For all its prophetic vagaries, however—what really,
in the last analysis, do East and West mean in it?—
there is a power of conviction to Nachman's speech
that leaves little room for doubt that the ideas in it
were Feierberg's own. There are few more remarka-
ble visions in early Zionist literature—and few that
seem more relevant even in their wrongness when
reread today.

That the final pages of "Whither?" have a rushed
and somewhat arbitrary quality compared to the
chapters that precede them was first noticed by
Ahad Ha'am, who did not, however, connect this fact
with Feierberg's failing health and his determination
to finish the novella while he still had the strength.
Feierberg had mailed him a completed draft of
"Whither?" in late December 1898, referring to it in
a brief letter as "a new experiment" and acknowl-
edging his indebtedness to Ahad Ha'am for some of
the thoughts expressed in it. Ahad Ha'am wrote back
within the week to say that he had read the story, and
continued:

> Your fundamental conception is excellent, but you
> lacked the patience to develop it fully to the end. At
> first you worked intensively . . . occasionally even
> expanding certain passages more than they deserved.
> Toward the end, however (starting with your hero's
> wedding), you seem to tire and to seek to be as brief
> as possible. In consequence, the final episode seems
> hurried and unconnected to what comes before, so
> that your hero's natural development suddenly
> jumps. . . . This is especially true of his conversation

with the freethinker, and even more so, of his final oration, both of which come as a surprise to the reader, who lacks a sense of their necessity.[13]

In this first version of "Whither?" Feierberg had autobiographically let Nachman die of complications resulting from a lung infection, to which Ahad Ha'am objected as well, observing that "His [Nachman's] death from a cold seems capricious in the extreme, as though it came merely to finish a story whose hero the author no longer knew what to do with." In sum, Ahad Ha'am concluded, the final section of the story needed additional work; since the length of the piece, however, necessitated its serialization in any case, he was willing to start publishing the opening chapters in *Hashiloah* while Feierberg was revising the last ones.

Feierberg's reply to this letter casts light both on the ending of "Whither?" and on his sense of his own situation at the time that he was writing it. After conceding that the novella had its structural faults, he went on:

> Your saying that "his [Nachman's] death from a cold seems capricious in the extreme, as though it came merely to finish a story whose hero the author no longer knew what to do with" seems unjustified to me. I ended the story as I did not because I didn't know "what to do" with my hero, but because my hero himself didn't know and was incapable of doing anything at all. . . . [Nachman] has pondered and thought a great deal, but for him to advance any further from where I have left him—this neither the circumstances of his life, nor of his education, nor of his social position would allow. A new generation is

needed for this, one raised on its own values and conceptions. It would be ludicrous for [Nachman] to pick himself up and head "eastward" himself. Such [would-be] "heroes," of which there is at present no lack in real life, must be made to realize that they themselves, however able they may be, cannot supply the [human] material needed for our [national] reconstruction. At best they can help prepare this material for the future. If my hero were of this common variety, he could have gone on living many years longer, but for a person of his aspirations, who is perfectly aware that the program he proposes is beyond his own powers, death is all to the good. If not for death, he would simply remain in his madness: even after surmounting his despair and finding an answer to his great question [of the future of the Jewish people], the enormity of his struggle and the adversity of his life have exhausted him to the point where he can no longer conceive of starting all over himself.

Nevertheless, he agreed to forgo Nachman's lungs as the cause of his death, which he rather perfunctorily disposed of instead in the novella's last lines. (Ahad Ha'am had suggested suicide, a solution that, given Feierberg's own condition at the time, must have seemed to him oddly inappropriate.) He also rewrote several passages toward the end of the story and strengthened the connecting links between them. In February 1899, shortly before his death, he mailed off a new draft of "Whither?"; the first part of the novella appeared in *Hashiloah* that same month, while three additional installments were published posthumously in the spring of the year.

While working on "Whither?" Feierberg had

conceived of yet another project, for which he was on the verge of gathering material at the time of his death. This was to be a novel about the eighteenth-century figure of the Baal Shem Tov, the semilegendary wonder-worker and founder of the Hasidic movement. In October 1898 he had written to a friend:

> The idea of this [novel] is so sacred and grand to me that I tremble to think that I might not see it through or that I might fail to take in all the many aspects [of the subject] that I have in mind. It is a disgrace to our people, to its degraded taste and enslavement to outward glitter, that a hundred books have not been written already about this most extraordinary movement (Hasidism, that is) and the great man who founded it . . . I hope to be objective without passing judgment and to see and penetrate to the inner core of things.[14]

The subject of the Baal Shem Tov—who, like the movement that he founded, had suffered unjustly from the rationalist and antimystical bias of the historians of the Haskalah school—was a natural one for Feierberg to pick, for besides offering a wealth of untapped popular folklore that might be put to fictional use, it would have enabled him to pursue his ambition of exploring the evolution of "those myths, manners, and customs that shape and influence our lives," as he had written to Ahad Ha'am the year before. The historical nature of the subject must have appealed to him too because of the extra step back from his material in time that it would have afforded him. It was this pursuit of perspective, indeed, of that power of objectification and control that is the mark of any true artist, while at the same time surrendering none of the intense emotion with which he wrote, that had steadily characterized his development from "Yankev the Watchman" until now. A novel about the Baal Shem Tov would have been the first work he had attempted that was not, in the strict sense, autobiographical, and that might have had some of the richness of mature fiction in which the imagination is free to fashion and shape a world all its own. He left no clue as to what the nature of the novel was to be; yet one can only assume that it would have gone beyond "Whither?" in much the same way that "Whither?" went beyond what came before. We are the poorer that he did not live to write it.

Hillel Halkin

N O T E S

1. The description is from the second of two "Letters from Volhynia" that Feierberg wrote for the Saint Petersburg *Hamelitz* in the autumn of 1896 and the following winter. The letters

were republished in the first edition of Feierberg's collected works, which appeared in Warsaw in 1904 with an introduction by the critic Yosef Klausner.

2. Setzer's brief memoir, the single most valuable source on Feierberg's life, was published in the 1903 literary supplement of the Warsaw *Hatsefirah* (*Me'asef li'shnat ha-sheloshim le-Hatsefirah, 2*). I am indebted to Yehuda Yaari of Jerusalem for his kindness in helping me to obtain a copy of this essay.

3. Of Feierberg's letters, only those to Ahad Ha'am have survived. They were published in the monthly *Me'oznayim*, 1928–29, vol. 1, nos. 19–22.

4. The essay first appeared in the 1904 edition of Feierberg's works.

5. Wohl's memoir, more fragmentary than Setzer's, appeared in *Hatsefirah*, 1900, nos. 55–56, and 1901, nos. 231–233.

6. Though Feierberg did not send "The Shadows" and the letter that accompanied it to *Hashiloah* until June 1897, all evidence points to its having been written the previous winter (see note 11). Most likely he did not wish to submit it for publication until he had heard of the fate of two other pieces of fiction that he had sent to *Hashiloah* in March, and with which his correspondence with Ahad Ha'am began. These stories, now lost, were probably identical with two unpublished manuscripts of Feierberg's called "Reflections of a Dying Heart" and "In Closing" that were seen by Shmuel Tsvi Setzer; the first of these, at least, was apparently written before "Yankev the Watchman" and may have been part of the material shown to Nachum Sokolov in Warsaw. Ahad Ha'am did not publish them, but his letter of rejection has been lost as well.

7. These were the two "Letters from Volhynia" published in *Hamelitz*.

8. The essay was submitted to *Hashiloah* in September of that year but never appeared there. It was first published in the 1904 collected works.

9. The collected letters of Ahad Ha'am, *Iggerot Ahad Ha'am*, 1: 110.

10. It appeared in the 1897–98 edition of the Warsaw literary annual *Luah Ahiasaf.*

11. Because Feierberg did not send "A Spring Night" to

Ahad Ha'am for publication until March 1898 (the story was rejected for *Hashiloah* and published along with "The Shadows" in the 1897–98 *Luah Ahiasaf*), when he submitted it together with "The Amulet," it has been assumed by such standard authorities as Klausner and Fishl Lachover (cf. his chapter on Feierberg in his *Toledot ha-Sifrut ha-Ivrit ha-Hadashah*) that the story was written after "The Calf" and "In the Evening." It is indeed unclear why Feierberg kept it as long as he did (possibly he feared at the time—quite rightly as it turned out—that it would be rejected like "The Shadows"), but it is obvious on textual grounds alone that "A Spring Night" is an earlier work than "The Calf," to say nothing of "In the Evening" and "The Amulet." Moreover, the atmospheric intensity of the story makes it hardly credible that it could have been written at any other time of year than spring, and since the spring of 1898 is out of the question, this leaves only that of 1897, after "The Shadows" and before "The Calf." Indeed, Feierberg's sensitivity to the seasons was such that not only "A Spring Night" but each story that he wrote bears the mark of the months in which it was composed. From descriptions of nature or references to weather alone we would know that "Yankev the Watchman" was written in late autumn or early winter, "The Shadows" in winter, "The Calf" in summer, and "In the Evening" and "The Amulet" in fall. True, the opening scene of "Whither?" is set on the Day of Atonement, that is, in late summer or early autumn, while the novella itself was begun in the spring; but this passage, which was in fact written in spring, is a "flash-forward" set out of chronological sequence, while the chapters that follow, though they take place over a period of many years, move in orderly fashion through summer to fall, the final scene of the story, that of Nachman's oration, occurring "one winter evening," just when we know that Feierberg was writing it.

12. The story was submitted to *Hashiloah* in November 1897, but was not published there until December 1898, after "The Amulet," which appeared in October of that year.

13. *Iggerot Ahad Ha'am*, 1: 228.

14. The letter is quoted by Yosef Klausner in his introduction to the 1904 collected works.

First
Stories

Yankev the
Watchman

And when the black bile rises within me at the sight of the tears of these damned;

Which I see and hear and stop my mouth with ashes because all hope is lost;

When I see that the sky above is of iron and the earth below is of steel and my place is halfway between them;

And I understand at last that there is nowhere to stand, or to lay my head, or to call my own, because the earth keeps shifting beneath me;

And that I am sentenced for life on this earth to be a bone in the throat which can neither be swallowed nor spit out;

And when I look through my peephole at this vast world—this great world which laughs at all smallness—this vast rock which lies beneath the eternally hammering sledge that eternally splits it into infinite fragments of stone and of sand—and I ask:

Lord of the universe! Why so much dust?

(This dust which has been scattered and carried to the ends of the earth until not a grain resembles the pebbles first placed on the pile: Why so much of it? To whom can it be any use?)

And when the bilious question seeps through the walls of my heart and corrodes my brain until I scratch and grub like a bat at the earth on my grave, from which the wild weeds grow already, to let in a glimmer of light from that great, vast enlightened world outside so that my dry bones and worn body may find the strength to live on:

Then the graves open up and the spectral apparitions of darkness swarm by the thousands and ten thousands before me—how awful these phantoms! how dreadful the death that lurks above these denizens of the deep!—and there is my answer among them: the strength to live on! Then the souls of the saints pass before me as though on review and I see down the corridors of time.

Then he too stands before me as real as life.

Who let him in among these immortals? Who joined this small link to the immemorial chain of holy souls that inspire such high reverence?

For was he not after all just a simple town watchman?

And again a memory from childhood. How good it is to remember!

He stands before me as real as life. I thought little enough of him then. I cared only for what was especially bright and shiny or especially pretty and soft. In those days I still saw God's angels following me wherever I went. Cherubs spread their wings above my head to shelter me with a canopy of peace and joy. I, child that I was, was a green new citizen of a sweet and gentle world. Why should I have taken notice of anyone like him?

He was a broad-shouldered, plain-featured fellow with a long, thick nose, a squat forehead, and saucer-shaped eyes in which shone neither particular intelligence nor particular cunning, neither the spontaneous enjoyment of life nor the sophistication thereof—eyes that had little to offer the physiognomist except for the history of suffering that looked out from them when he talked about himself. Then they almost made one think of a hero defying all odds on a field of war.

And he truly was a hero at that.

Though not the only one of his kind among his people.

Others too had fallen like him by the wayside.

Others too had risen like him from the dead.

Others too had come and had gone in darkness.

And who will mourn for them all? Who will speak for these weather-beaten, plain-featured thousands and ten thousands of our fellow Jews who came and went in darkness to be the atoning victims for our Jewish folly?

He was still a boy in his father's house when he heard the melancholy cry in the night:

"Woe that the Shekhinah is in exile!"

Throughout the long winter nights he lay with his father on the straw mattress. The pale snow sparkled outside the low window and the elegant moon stared straight at his bed and trembled with cold, its wan rays sweeping the ledge of the stove where his three sisters slept with his mother. The bitter frost kept him awake. From time to time he rubbed himself all over, squirming and curling and fondly hugging his hands to his body. When he was warmed he felt better and he lay there enjoying the pleasuresome sensation.

Yet sometimes he wondered whether it was really the moon that trembled with cold on the ledge of the stove or his mother and sisters, and the thought made him sad.

And sometimes his father would wake from his sleep with a seizure of coughing.

He watched him light a candle and sit down with it on the floor.

His long shadow stretched elastically until it took in the length of the room. It fell on the frost-covered pile of potatoes that lay in one corner and rocked darkly back and forth, its head bobbing up and down above the pile.

He was holding a midnight vigil.

His voice flowed forth with mellifluous sadness. He was crying. How beauteous the hot tears that fell from his chill eyes; how precious the gemlike drops that sparkled like sapphires inlaid in the strands of his white beard; how intense the living sadness that emanated from his thin, cadaverous frame. . . .

His cough was dreadful. It seemed to come from some rock bottom of the soul. And the shadows rocked, rocked back and forth, like harbingers of death.

He crooned melodically, his voice rising and falling. Sometimes it seemed pregnant with longing, his soul a tender young thing that poured itself forth in a fury of fancy for the precious object of its love, toward which it strove boldly with the vigor of youth, for which it waited trustingly with the innocence of youth. Then the shadow swayed calmly and his cadaverous face shone by the candle's dim light.

But sometimes his voice trembled badly and he let out a horrible groan of self-denying, life-denying despair. How hopeless! His black shadow darted swiftly about the room and the storm inside him erupted in a cough.

It blew itself out with a bitter sigh and he cried from the depths of his heart:

"Woe that the Shekhinah is in exile!"

The boy lay there all ears. He didn't know what was happening or understand a word of the holy prayer book that lay open before his father; he didn't even stop to think that he should; but he was overcome with emotion. He felt powerfully bound to his father and his chant. It made him want to cry . . . it made him want to laugh . . . it made him . . . but *who* was he really, anyway?

It cut a channel deep within him, there where "the raven-black song that resounds like an angelic voice from high Horeb's ruins" lay buried.

In the mornings he sat with his sisters on top of the stove and ate hot, delicious potatoes. Feeling warm and happy and contented, he remembered the night before when his father's sad voice had seemed stronger and more insistent than ever. He remembered the words "woe," "exile," and Shekhinah, which he often had heard from his mother as well. And his elder sister too, when she had been sick, had screamed something that sounded like "woe" before she died. From then on he liked to hum the sad words to himself out loud as though they were music.

Before his eleventh birthday his father died.

He was determined to be a good father to his three younger sisters and a source of comfort and strength to his widowed mother.

Yet she knew that he was only a boy and she lifted her eyes to the Father of all, the protector of orphans and widows.

It was then that he was offered up on the hellish altar by the high priests of his people.

The high priests?

Say not a word! The earth will yet quake and the pillars of heaven crash down at their mention. In those cannibal days, when this holy people, this worm of Jacob, divided itself in back rooms into the chosen of God and the chosen of man, and the first dragged the second to the altar of Moloch, which it had built for its fellow Jews created in God's image no less than itself, and offered them up in its stead, this destitute orphan, this only son, this mother's sole worldly support, was fraudulently impressed into the army of the czar to ransom the seven sleek sons of some wealthy Jew.

Lord God! Was it too much for Your pure eyes that You saw no evil but held Your tongue and kept silent at the hideous sight? You show Your mercy on the nest of a sparrow; Your righteousness and kindness are as mighty mountains; and how could You not have pitied this family of misfortune that sat downtrodden at the city gate and found no redeemer?

That day a new stream of tears poured into the great tearful ocean that circles our Jewish world and mingled with the drops that many another family of Israelites had shed.

It was a winter night.

The moon was concealed in its heavenly mansion, over which dark, black strips of watery cloud had been draped as though to chastise it from seeing the face of the earth and keep it from quitting its place of hiding to light up the globe and its dwellers. Unnoticed among those deprived of its rays, a wretched young lad, a weak, helpless boy who had never before set foot by himself from his home after dark, now lay all alone, bound hand and foot in the town dungeon.

And the shadows! The pale satyrs, the white ghosts, the old cantor who rose every night from his grave wrapped in white shrouds to recite the public prayer in the synagogue as though he had never died; Treyna the fortune-teller who had once stuck her tongue out from the women's gallery of the synagogue all the way to its eastern wall to lick a pinch of tobacco from the snuffbox that the beadle had taken out of his pocket; the old wizard, the apostate washerwoman, the sinful virgin, Asmodai king of the demons, his own dead, pale-faced sister: all rose together from the ground disguised as red and black dots and perched above his nose, where they grew bigger and larger by the minute, changing shape over and over until they finally assumed their true form. In his ears rang a sound like that of a small, distant bell. The larger the figures became, the more clearly it rang. It grew louder and louder, until the motley company began to dance, circling around the room above his head. Then he heard a wild laugh and the figures grew smaller and shrank back to dots, while the sound of the bell grew distant and faint once again. Now he saw his father sitting in the corner and nodding his head as he did when he was still alive and rose for the midnight vigil. "Woe that the Shekhinah is in exile!" he exclaimed, half unconsciously chanting the words he had learned from him. His fear vanished and he felt a wave of relief.

A few days later he was shipped to a distant province.

His life there? Where is the mind that can grasp the millions and trillions of infinitely minute details that change from minute to minute, from place to place, that are now the cause and now the effect, all in accordance with what, when, and where?

And these same details, which were entered one after another like figures on a palimpsest from which the old was continually erased to make room for the new, relentlessly eroded memories, customs, and habits from the surface of our hero's mind and altered his life, his appearance, and even his language. Yet all was not blotted out—and sometimes at night he still cried out in his bed:

"Woe that the Shekhinah is in exile!"

Then he felt a ray of new light pierce the darkness of his soul.

Summertime.

The goodly sun had just cleared the horizon to embrace fair nature with its golden rays, spreading life and light everywhere and refreshing the spirit of man, when our hero too awoke from his slumber along with the drowsy earth to find himself couched in a field by the flock with which his master had entrusted him.

A light breeze blew over the cover of grass where the flock had been grazing and passed lightly on, gently shaking the trees in the nearby forest. The whole meadow hummed with breathless music, melodious and sweet. . . .

Every leaf, each blade of grass, bowed down in a paean of praise before the Creator!

And when all creation, from the lowliest bush to the tallest tree, had burst into song, could man keep from singing too?

(Does it not indeed sometimes seem as though creation sang through the fountainhead of man's soul alone? Who else can read God's score at a glance and arrange the notes into the magnificent symphony of existence that we see?)

And so he sang too, for his soul was nature's child that awoke with the passing breeze.

The waves of sound were wafted on the wings of the wind through the glorious air. A thousand voices echoed the refrain, and the trees of the forest waved their green leaves in applause.

How banal seem the actor's arts, how contemptible the singer's trained voice, how mean and unappreciative their audiences, when compared with a stage, a singer, and an audience like these!

How great would be the singer who could imitate just once the song of the lark!

How sublime would be the poet who could plumb to its depths the soul of an innocent youth!

And yet these feats too would be mere photographs, the shadows of the image of the poem itself.

And the poem itself?

The boy sang!

The waves of sound were wafted on the wings of the wind; a thousand voices echoed the refrain; the leaves of the forest applauded as he sang.

His song coursed through his veins to his heart and his mind. How strangely it affected him there! It brought out hidden feelings that he couldn't describe. He recalled that the very language in which he was singing had been unknown to him five years before . . . suddenly a gate swung open in the halls of his heart and he stepped through it and into infinite worlds, soaring and gliding from the chasms of the abyss to the highest heavens, feeling free at last.

The boy sang!

The waves of sound were wafted on the wings of the wind and a thousand voices echoed the refrain:

"Woe that the Shekhinah is in exile!"

The birch rods that existed in those days of serfdom, before the imperial throne let its merciful light shine upon the peasant:

Who better than the Jew knew the taste of them and their lasting effect upon the mangled back of a man?

How many noble and upright spirits were humbled by its fearful rain of blows!

On that distant day to come when unscarred

human beings will write the history of mankind's awakening; on that far-off day whose light we only now see dawning in the east when poets will lament the hurt of the smallest fly tormented in the spider's web; on that day humankind will shed torrents of tears to hear of such long-ago things, like the torrents of blood that were spilled by the birch itself.

More than once he suffered under its lash while indentured to some landowner.

Like a hero, without flinching, he fought the good, the difficult battle for his own soul.

The redeeming winds of change that blew from the palace of the new czar throughout the vast land, abolishing serfdom and cleansing human society from the stains of prejudice and the delusions of darkest ignorance, brought pardon and clemency, justice and mercy to all his subjects and dispatched in a day what his ancestors had debated doing for generations.

Then our hero returned to his native village to become a night watchman.

I was just a small boy at the time.

It was autumn. The mud and mire were neck-high. The sky was covered with thick, dark clouds. Up before the crack of dawn, I set out for the heder with my lantern in hand.

It was utterly still in the streets. The town was shrouded in silence. Now and then the watchmen making their rounds called out of the night to each other. And among them I heard a not unfamiliar voice as it cried:

"Woe that the Shekhinah is in exile!"

It was the voice of Yankev the Watchman.

A corpse lay on a stretcher before me.

A few men accompanied it. The funeral passed quickly. There were no cries, no sighs, no tears, no sorrowful words. The handful of men dwindled and disappeared.

Quickly the corpse was laid in its eternal home to return to the dust from whence it came.

Who was it?

Yankev the Watchman!

The
Shadows

*. . . yet in all this wide world with its many fair
pleasures—in this life of infinite spectacles and
amusements—nothing has taken my fancy but darkness alone.*

*Many are the lovers of daytime and sunlight;
but I have been the lover of nighttime and dark.*

*A black shadow on a moonless night—is there
anywhere a finer sight?*

*How the cruel sun hurts my eyes! The blustering
light bids me see and enjoy its stale, unprofitable,
odious world. With each fleeting moment, new diver-
sion, base desire, my fickle heart stirs and rushes to*

enter where it was never made to tread. A hell opens
beneath it into which it sinks deep down, dragging
me bodily after it, even as I move and feel. Bound
against my will to this world of sham, kept from the
shadows I love by my wild, licentious heart—blissful
now in the sorcerous sunshine—my thoughts turn
back one last time, alas! . . . to the dark.

Nighttime.

I was in the old, crumbling study house. The sun
had already gone down and a storm wind wailed and
whistled outside, rattling the broken windowpanes
and toying with the flame of the candle in my hand,
which it vigorously cuffed back and forth. The lecterns scattered about the building were softly out-
lined like tombstones over graves. I stood leaning
against one of them in the middle of the large room,
an old Talmud, over which I pored, before me.

My little candle burned with a thin crackle and
spattered spots of tallow on the Talmud. The dim
light that it cast filled the building with dusky shadows. It flitted around me for a few square feet and
then ascended through the darkness, which rose too
from the four sepulchrally black corners of the study
house to spread over the ceiling above, before falling
like a curtain halfway down the drapery of the holy
ark that stood in front of me. The shadows swayed
back and forth, interweaving and overlapping. The
whole house seemed to sway too. The walls bowed
low. The shadows exchanged friendly greetings and
embraced when they met. I could see them whisper,
what I didn't know, because they whispered in silence and I couldn't hear.

I played hide-and-seek with them, concealing them in my body as though inhaling them deeply, delighted with their blackness. I would have liked them to be even blacker, to spread far and wide and flood the world with the same sweet terror, the delicious fear, with which they filled me.

The Talmud lay open before me. I studied out loud, chanting the text in a voice mournful enough to wake the dead. The shadows listened and began to dance. My heart kept time to the beat, for the chant had slipped through its defenses and ensconced itself there uninvited.

I, Hofni, didn't know what it was that I felt. I couldn't understand my own self. I couldn't make out the least of the thousands of powers that ruled over me and harmonized among themselves in moments of happiness like this. I was determined to make a supreme effort to understand myself better, to save at least a few sketchy memories of this beatific hour from oblivion.

For the first time I realized how drawn I was to the dark. It was these shadows who had lured me to the study house in the dead of night in the first place; it was they who had cast their bittersweet spirit over the Talmud, they who had composed this melancholy chant; they, only they . . .

But who were they? And what were they to me?

My father had once told me how as a youngster he had loved to spend nights in the study house immersed in the Talmud. It had been his one pleasure in a life full of disappointment. I recalled how when he had spoken of these memories and of his powers of youthful devotion, tears of longing had come to his eyes for the wonderful nights spent in the service of the Law in the study house. At such times, he said, he had felt as though an unearthly spirit had been loosed on him from on high, striking his heart with God's holy firebolt and flooding him inwardly with a warm glow of love for the dark, for the night, for his own plaintive chant. Who was to say that it wasn't the same dark, the same night, the same chant that I loved too? Perhaps it was after all my one inheritance from my father. . . .

My poor, happy father! *You* never quenched your heart's holy fire with that other, alien flame of desire. You never squandered your warmth in the cold sea of life. You, father, suppressed each desire before it could make itself known—while in me, your unhappy son, fire fought against fire. The sea of life raged around my heart, each desire yielding only to a fresher and fiercer one. My will was enslaved to hard masters. All the ill winds that howled through the world had come home to roost in my heart. Day by day I could see the kingdom of shadows losing its sway over me and the holy spirit departing.

The world slept while I woke.

I knew it didn't envy my happiness. It was the slugabeds who thought they were the happy ones; the small, self-satisfied souls who rejoiced over each piece of bread as though it were a treasure that they had risked their lives to find, toiling by day to eat and sleep by night, and eating and sleeping by night to toil by day; the pleasure-hunters and all-night-revelers, sunk in the wretched quicksands of desire, drunken with lust and every loathsome entertain-

ment; all shook their heads sadly at the likes of me.
And I too sometimes felt the unaccustomed urge to
ask myself: "Hofni, you fool, what are you doing
here? Why must you banish sleep from your eyes and
pleasure from your flesh?" Yet I knew that I was
happy, the happiest of men. The day my happiness
came to an end would be the day I went to bed at the
same time as everyone else, the day I chased after
phantoms like an ordinary man, the day . . . when
"the day breatheth, and the shadows flee away."

I knew that in the world's eyes my study house
was an old, deserted, dilapidated ruin. But I would be
steadfast!

The whole world was but a speck in my heart,
which was but a speck in the old study house. Let the
sun go out and the world would darken too. . . .

Then I would see my study house standing at the
center of creation, the spokes of light streaming from
it all over the earth. . . .

And at night . . .

If ever I felt strangely moody or under an invisi-
ble spell that called on me to follow I didn't know
where, if ever my soul craved refreshment that was
not to be got in the pantry, if ever my tear-laden eyes
sought a gentle flower on which to tender their dew,
then it was to the study house that I fled, to dally
away the time with my company of shadows, by the
dim candle, before the holy books.

For the holy books were holy for sure . . . and the
cases of them, how full!

I never knew how it happened, but it did: there
were times when I didn't see those books at all, but
armies of men, generations on parade. How tall and

majestic they looked, how their faces shone with light! Out of the old bookcases they stepped, to mingle with the shadows black. Freshets, rivers of blood flowed beneath them. Their cries and groans reached the heavens. Behind them, before them, were rivers of salt tears and blood . . . behind and before me too. . . .

Salt tears and blood!

And in the bloody, crushed, mangled bodies that dangled above the abyss, what noble, what holy souls! Salt tears and blood!

I wasn't alone here; many were as unhappy as I; I could see nothing but wasteland and wilderness before me, nothing but darkness and depths behind . . . No, I wasn't alone; many were as happy as I; I could see only light and goodness before me, only eternal splendor behind. Here . . . but how large the world seemed from here!

Here I would live and die. Here I would suffer, as each of these shades rising toward me from the old cases of books must have suffered. Here I would hope, as they must have hoped in their anguish.

Out of the whirlwind of frighteningly bitter thoughts that lashed at my mind and cast a black cloud over me—at the sight of these awful immortals, of their shame and degradation, of their agonies of body and spirit—I felt a fierce pride to know that these miserable thousands had endured and survived all the same: survived all those who had plotted their ruin, endured amid the faded, mildewed pages in these rotting cases of books.

And yet . . .

How difficult and deep the Talmud was! The

commentary of the Maharsha, it was said, built whole worlds and destroyed them—but what kind of worlds did it build? How puny and narrow they were, what patchwork! And there were the commentaries of Alfasi, of Mordecai, of Reb Asher, of Maimonides, of the *Tur*, of Rabbi Joseph Caro too. I had dived into a vast and infinite sea—but what would I find at the bottom?

And yet there was also *The Kuzari, The Guide to the Perplexed, The Beliefs and Opinions, The Wars of the Lord.* How I loved *The Kuzari* and *The Guide!*

Except that my father . . . ah, my father!

My father said that it was sinful even to look at *The Guide.* "Get your fill of the Talmud," he had told me. "Our minds hold only so much, and the Evil Urge lies in wait to entrap us at every step. Please, son, think of me and of your own soul: don't spend your time on that siren Philosophy. . . ."

"What ever is the matter with you?" asked my mother. "What makes you take such nonsense seriously? Your father never bothered with philosophy and neither did your grandfather. In our whole family we never had a single philosophizer. And your future father-in-law isn't one either. He's a successful, well-liked man, and your bride to be is as pretty as the moon and as pure as sunshine. This coming Purim they'll send you a gold watch for sure. . . ."

The Guide, The Guide! How awesome it was. And how I loved it.

It made me shiver all over. It was hair-raising to think that there were thoughts as high as the heavens and as deep as a bottomless gulf. And alone in this realm of intellect I was forced to wander by myself, swept against my will by a powerful tide into an odious world where I had to think and think all the time. . . .

They were frighteningly bitter, these thoughts. They bore into my brain and gave it no rest; they cracked open my bones and sucked at the living marrow. Two worlds were at war inside me, as different as east was from west, and my poor heart had to manage with both. . . .

There was a knock at the door. It was certain to be Reb Shlomo. Every week he spent three waking nights in the study house. I quickly hid *The Guide* underneath the lectern, because Reb Shlomo didn't approve of it. "I'm for the Maimonides who wrote *The Strong Hand*," he'd once told me, "but not for the Maimonides who wrote *The Guide*." And because I loved Reb Shlomo dearly, I wouldn't have hurt his feelings for the world.

Reb Shlomo was a portrait of luminous brightness among the black shadows that cavorted in the study house.

He was a stooped old man of sixty or more with a head that sunk in on his chest. His wide, pale expanse of forehead was crisscrossed with large and small gullies, beneath which his large, deep eyes squinted lightly like two mountain ponds among craggy hills crowned with thick woods. A lingering smile, the outcome of some profound reflection of love and goodwill toward his fellowman, played on his lips, while both the innocence of youth and the calm of old age looked out from his face.

He had an intense, magnetic effect on me. Could it be, I would ask myself, that this tower of learning,

this Sinai who could move mountains with his knowledge, this oppressed, penniless soul who hadn't a
thing to eat or to wear in his house—could it be that
he should stay awake through the night, while I, a
boy in my prime, I, who had never had to worry
where my next meal was coming from, should want
to sleep? What a sorry figure I seemed to myself at
such times!

Reb Shlomo preferred to study on his feet. When
he was seated, he said, he didn't have the same feeling of devotion. The Torah, he said, demanded that
one put aside one's physical nature. It was not
enough for the self to forget that it was hungry or
tired. It had to forget what hunger and tiredness
were; it had to forget that there was a world and a life
apart from the world and the life of study; it had to
forget that its study had a beginning and an end; it
had to remember that it had been created for a purpose, and that it was but a link in the great, infinite
chain of the Law, whose only purpose was itself.

And Reb Shlomo forgot all these things, forgot
them completely. I swear by the blackened walls of
the old study house, which saw the stooped old man
bend over a Talmud on many a long winter night,
from evening till morning, that he truly forgot. . . .

I envied him then. I could tell by the glow on his
face that he was rapturously off in a world of his own.
There was nothing else that he wished for, nothing
that he cared for besides what he already had, which
he wanted only to enhance and improve.

You were actually a happy man, Reb Shlomo.

But I was far from that. I felt hemmed in on all
sides here. It was so dark I could hardly breathe.

. . . Life moved at a crawl. The blood coursed slug-
gishly in my veins. My soul tilted at phantasms and
old graves. I would never get out. It wasn't possible.
I could never leave the shadows that I loved. Their
world meant too much to me. I knew that beyond
this funereal room there was another world filled
with treasures. But they were kept under lock; no
eye had beheld them; and I was left looking for the
keys. . . .

The Guide and *The Kuzari* had sought the keys
too. They too had felt how cramped the study house
was, how its desolate wastes were no cure for life's
ills, how one needed to know more than ever it offered—but had they found it in the end? No, they had
simply made the house a bit larger; they had let in
more light; but the keys to the wide world beyond
had eluded them too. . . .

But who was this? I had been wrong. It wasn't
Reb Shlomo at all. An indigent traveler was standing
before me with a pack on his back.

"Good evening."

"A good evening to you!"

"Where can you be coming from, friend, in the
middle of the night?"

"I set out for the city this morning from a village
nearby. The peasants told me that it was only a three-
hour walk, and so I didn't eat or drink before I left,
because I said to myself, when I get to town I'll have
a bite among Jews. But the snow was so deep that I
lost my way, until I finally made it to here."

"Do you mean to say that you haven't eaten all
day? Why, you must think it's a fast day!"

"Ah, you're a lucky boy, you are! I can see that

you come from a comfortable home, or perhaps even a rich one, and so you can ask: 'Do you mean to say you haven't eaten?' Even a fast in the short days of winter must be an ordeal for you, and that though you spend it at home and know that a tasty meal is waiting for you in the evening when it's over. But we poor folk are used to going hungry. I'm fasting here and my wife and five boys are fasting back there. We poor folk are used to putting up with all kinds of hardship and humiliation, to being outcasts among men. . . . You're lucky, my boy, that you don't know what it means to be poor! Ah, if only you knew what it meant . . . if only you knew. . . ."

"But you must be hungry!"

"And what can I do if I am? Rouse sleepers from their beds? They step on me like a spider even when I leave them alone, and you want me to rob them of their precious sleep?"

It was deathly quiet outside. The silence lay spread all around. There wasn't a sound or a light. Only at the far end of the street, where a faint beam fell on the sidewalk, could I make out the voices of merrymakers.

I approached the house, traversed the entrance-way, and pushed hard against the door without giving it much thought.

It was all I could do. I had to get into the house. The poor traveler was hungry . . . and hunger was a terrible thing . . . in any case, I didn't imagine that it could be pleasant. Yes, I would enter no matter what . . . already I was standing in the drawing room.

It was a large, spacious room. Everything was

arranged in fine order. The chairs and tables were neatly set out. Elegant curtains covered the windows. A large chandelier suspended from the middle of the ceiling cast a clear, cheerful light on the tables. More light came from several large candles in silver holders. A crowd of men sat around in high spirits, amusing themselves at dice.

The flood of light and the din that greeted my ears after the limitless darkness and silence outside left no room for doubt that I had entered another world of other people and other lives. How warm and attractive it seemed! There wasn't a patch of darkness, not a shadow. Everything glittered brightly here, where the waves of life's sea broke with a thunderous crash to the sound of loud laughter.

Ah, life, life! I too was in love with it. I felt a warm flush inside me where the far poles of the earth, heaven and hell, were locked in furious combat.

I looked curiously at the people around me. I wanted to see right through them; I wanted to find out for myself how they thought, loved, and hated; I wanted to know whether there was any relation between the ambitious theory of freedom and the way it worked out in raw practice; I wanted to see whether they really lived by what they felt and believed in, or whether, alas, they simply felt and believed in however they happened to live; I wanted to know if they were at peace with themselves and their world; I wanted to see, to find out . . . perhaps here was the solution to the riddle . . . perhaps here was the sought-after shore, the source of the happy and the good . . . perhaps it was here that I must look for the answers to the questions that were torment-ing me. . . .

"Excuse me!"

The gathering looked up.

"What do you want, boy?" someone asked.

"What are you doing here, boy?" another inter-rupted.

"What are you looking for?" called out someone else.

"Come over here, boy!" a mocking voice cried.

"A very poor man just came to the study house. He was lost all day on the roads, and now he's tired and hungry, because he hasn't eaten all day. Please, gentlemen, have pity on him and give him some-thing to eat."

"Give him something to eat for his beggar man!"

"What are you doing in the study house, boy?"

"Are there really still idlers and rebels against the light sitting in the study house?"

"O ye dwellers in darkness!"

"Let us have a curl from one of your earlocks and we'll give you a piece of bread for your beggar."

"Tell us which of the girls here you like the most!"

A serving girl brought me a slice of bread and I left.

It was then that they fell in my eyes and seemed like insects to me. What vileness, I thought. If you're living beings, where are your feelings? Where is your sense of compassion? No, you're not living beings at all. There's more life and vitality in one wretched tear than in all your waltzes and meaningless amusements; a single one of old Reb Shlomo's thoughts lights up the dark crannies of the broken heart more than all the chandeliers and rotten glitter with which you fill your homes. . . . He—old Reb Shlomo, poor Reb Shlomo, weak Reb Shlomo, Reb Shlomo the butt of your jokes—has learned to transcend his wretched, foul, impoverished existence for another, loftier world where all is noble and holy. Wherever he cries—there is the deepest abyss. Wherever he hopes—there is the highest heaven. Wherever he wills—there is the entire cosmos. And you? How petty you are, what mere pieces of men, living in your vile little world of vile appetites and loathsome desires. . . .

I stood among the shadows again. The darkness brushed against me. I was left still seeking the way to a wider, airier world. I loved the darkness but I loved the sunlight even more . . . yet only the light of that sun which rose to shine on all . . . that sun which the highest, steepest walls couldn't cause to cast a shadow . . . that sun of good works which shone on the great and the small. Then I would leave my study house for good, I would put the shadows behind me.

But where to now? Where could I turn? To whom could I go?

Back to them who had spurned a suffering soul?

No. I didn't want to be with the oppressed. But even less did I want to be with—the oppressor.

A Spring Night

Old age is already upon me. My hair is gray now and my back is bent. I'm no longer the man I used to be.

And still all I've had my fill of are sorrow and spleen. It's not the weight of the years that has bent my back so but my own misspent, burdensome life.

There are times when I don't know whether to laugh or cry. In any case, there are no tears left. My feelings have long turned to stone. There isn't a curse in God's book that He hasn't brought down on me, and I can't even bring myself to sigh.

And yet I remember an evening when I was still an impressionable boy.

It was one of the first nights of spring.

An oil lamp burned dimly in my little room. My books lay before me in disorder on the table: the tractate Bava Kama, *The Kuzari, Yoreh De'ah,* Part I, *The Guide to the Perplexed, The Beginnings of Wisdom,* and a Bible. Several other, forbidden Hebrew books were hidden beneath the pillow on my bed.

A terrible feeling of sadness bore down on me. I brooded dimly in the dim light. The scattered pile of books on the table made me savagely moody.

I went to the window and flung it wide open.

All was quiet outside. The Street of the Jews was asleep. The shutters were drawn on the low windows. Here and there a thin ray of light bore through a crack to announce that some craftsman was still hard at work or some scholar immersed in a book. "The house cannot stand in which the words of the Law are not heard after dark"—and what indeed did a Jew find sweeter than midnight study?

A glorious, full-faced moon floated innocently in a sea of blue, flooding the street with a pale, pleasant light. A shaft of it fell on my window and on me looking out. Millions of stars twinkled and winked in the gorgeous dome of the sky. Aurorae pulsed softly in the vast night. A gentle breeze swept a distant fragrance into the street. Never had nature seemed so fresh, peaceful, and alive. Creation was one wonderful melody. Sweet sounds filled the air. Give thanks to the Lord for He is good, for His kindness is forever and ever. Holy of holies!

Here in this temple, where there were no books, manuscripts, theories, philosophies, cerebral wrinkles, or grandiloquent thoughts, God had made everything simple and straight.

I breathed the mild air as deeply as I could. What pleasure! My chest swelled, my heart pumped away . . . I lifted my eyes to the beautiful stars, to the moon in its sea-blue depths. . . . O God, God! How wonderful Your world was! How peaceful and majestic You had made it! How good it was to be alive amid such majesty on a superb night like this and to delight under Your skies!

And here in the street?

Your world was so holy and stupendous, God! The magnificent moon drifting on high, its face beaming with peace and love . . . the magical music of the spheres that came echoing down to me from your domed, mystic vaults . . . the splendor, the wonder, with which your universe was filled . . . what a vast, plentiful world it was! How much delicate pleasure and holy enjoyment could be had from it!

And here in the street?

Besides the shops and taverns, synagogues and study houses, schoolrooms and marketplace, there was God's world too: a world of moon and stars, of air and light, of deep blue skies and spring nights, of song birds and poems of grass, of overpowering emotions and arias of the soul. . . .

But here in the street?

"The meadows are clothed with flocks; the valleys also are covered over with corn; they shout for joy, yea, they sing"—I had never felt so fond of such verses before. The Talmud, the books of the moralists, codifiers, and commentators, had been my food for thought. I knew them as well as the street on which I lived. The Book of Psalms, the works of the philosophers, were all the poetry in my life. It was from them that I knew that the valleys were covered with corn and that "springs are sent forth into the valleys; they run between the mountains; they give drink to every beast of the field, the wild asses quench their thirst." But the valleys, the corn, the springs, the mountains themselves I had never once seen.

It was silent all around. I felt a tingling in my ears. Something was pressing on me. I felt so constricted . . . what was it that made me suddenly want to cry? What were all these tears about? So terribly constricted! Where had my childhood gone? Was this my life? What kind of world was I living in? O God!

Had I ever really known what it meant to be young, to be fully alive? Had I ever felt in the springtime of my youth what every tree, bush, flower, plant, fly, insect, bird on the wing felt in this springtime of the year?

What a gift it was to be young. Everywhere men were blooming with nature in the prime of their youth.

And I, here in the street?

Far down the street nature bloomed, youth blossomed, trees broke into bud, cheeks flushed red.

And here?

Life in Your world, God, was brimming with innocence, goodness, happiness, contentment. How many tens of thousands of souls were now enjoying the bounteous blessings You had given them! How many tens of thousands of hearts were bursting with peace and serenity, faith and trustfulness, prayer and thanksgiving! How many tens of thousands of young nerves were thrilling with loving longing for the exquisite pleasures of life!

Life, life, life! O God, life!

And here in the street?

Here in the street, in this anthill on which no sun ever rose, no moon ever shone, and no stars ever sparkled; on which nature never bloomed and life was never lived; on which a fierce, bitter battle was being fought by life against life in the name of life; here all that mattered was to get through the horror of life as quickly as one could. Even the crowning glories of life, the human eye and the human heart, were considered superfluous here, mere panders of sin. O ye miserable creatures: let your eyes see not and your hearts desire not! But what was there to see and what was there to desire here in the street?

I saw bent backs, pale faces, fallen cheeks, craggy beards, furrowed brows, glittering eyes set into ruins. These eyes wanted to see, they *could* see . . . hearts beat with desire here too . . . but what could their monkish possessors know of all that was seen and desired in the vast world outside, beyond the walls of their hermitage?

How could the worm underground have any way of knowing that just a foot above its head life went gaily on in the sunlight?

The avenue of green trees in the distance was a glorious sight. How pretty the young leaves were! I looked at them fondly, recalling the marvelous shade they had given through last summer's heat. I felt a terrible weight on my heart. My feelings were in a turmoil. I wanted to get out . . . I wanted to walk by myself, alone with the moon, among the avenues of trees. . . .

I stepped outside.

There wasn't a sound in the street. All was quiet. The pressure on my heart grew worse. Life, nature, these avenues of trees were all beyond me, far down the street.

I heard a dog bark far down the street.

I—

in the middle of the street.

Tales of
Hofni

The
Calf

It was summertime, and I wasn't yet nine years old.

The sun looking down from its station overhead bore into the gloomy heder with fiery eyes. As though to put our teacher to shame, it glanced scornfully off the protruding fringes of his dirty undershawl and ran teasing rays through his pointy beard. It poured playfully golden beams over the muddy morass by the open sewer that ran along the Street of the Poorhouse, which was also the Street of the Synagogue, as well as the Street of the Tutors, the Street of the Slaughterers, and the Street of the Mar-

ketplace, as if to say in so many laughing, magical
words: "You silly children! What makes you sit all
cooped up like this with such an old fool of a rabbi?"
How dearly we loved them then, those spinning sunbeams that twirled through the window with the
fondest of ease. It was a clear, balmy day outside.
What fun could be had there! The vapors rising from
the sewer made a fine sight; a scrimmage of boys was
having a jolly time wrestling on the ground and making mud pies to dry in the sun. But the hardhearted
rabbi refused to reprieve us and sat droning on and
on. Beads of sweat fell on the open Talmud. Our
damp shirts clung to our skins. Our hands felt leaden;
our heads ached; our throats were hoarse; but the
rabbi droned on and on. . . .

Yet even he had his breaking point. He finally
shut his book, admonished us with a few brief words,
and warned us to go straight to the synagogue for the
afternoon and evening prayer. In a frenzy of impa-
tience we tumbled outside—to be met by the town
herd coming toward us. First came the billy goats,
looking as stately and staid as a delegation of rabbis
and town notables on their way with the common
folk to attend some celebration, a wedding perhaps,
or a circumcision or a funeral. Next came the she-
goats, followed by the cows, calves, pigs, and colts,
each in a formation of their own. The dust rose sky
high. We slipped and scrambled in and out of the
herd, here someone stealing a ride on a billy goat's
back and there on a she-goat's, while yet someone
else terrorized the animals by stampeding them
wildly to let them know he was a man, a scion of that
heroic race whose dominion was one with the world.

Suddenly, at the herd's edge, I spied our own cow coming toward me by the side of the herdsman, who was carrying a lovely little calf on one shoulder. I put two and two together at once, for my mother had mentioned several times that our cow was "expecting." I couldn't contain my excitement, and I stared longingly at the herdsman as he strode toward my father's house with the pretty calf on his shoulder. I wanted desperately to run after him, to throw myself ardently on the calf and cover it with kisses, but what was I to do? What about the rabbi and the afternoon prayer? And what would my mother say if she were to see her son the Talmud student giving in to such unworthy impulses? And so I had no choice but to force myself to go to the synagogue to pray. As soon as the service was over, I rushed home to see the calf. My little sisters and brother ran out to greet me with news of the calf's birth when I came. "Hofni," they said all at once, "you should see how pretty it is! You should see how big its head is, and how wide its nostrils are, and how long its tongue is, and how red and thick its lips are! You should see . . ." Unable to restrain myself any longer, I ran impatiently to the barn, where I knelt before the calf on my knees and ran both hands over each of its limbs; then I took it in my arms and carried it to the kitchen to see it better by candlelight. I salted a few crumbs of bread and laid them on its tongue; it lapped them up hungrily and looked at me with a satisfied, genial air. I knew right then that it liked me and wanted to make friends with me more than with any of the other children, my brother and sisters too. It had eyes for me only, which followed me fondly wherever I went.

I fell madly, proudly in love with the pretty calf and pledged myself heart and soul to be good to it and to repay its devotion with my own.

"Well," said my mother to my father when he came home that evening, "we're in luck! The cow gave birth. We'll slaughter the calf next week and roast it the way you like it for the Sabbath."

"Do you mean it, mama?" I asked in alarm. "Do you really mean you'd kill such a nice, pretty calf?"

"You're still a child, son, and you're just being foolish. People would laugh at you if you talked that way in front of them."

When I returned from the kitchen to visit my calf, my pride and my joy, and saw it lift its eyes to me as though suing for mercy, I burst into tears. I threw myself on it passionately and stroked its sides while the hot tears trickled down my throat. The more I kissed it, the harder I cried.

That night, I remember, I couldn't stop thinking.

For the first time I felt as though a little bird were hatching inside my brain and pecking away with its sharp bill. . . . "Hofni!" I seemed to hear it say. "Why was such a calf ever made? To be slaughtered? But what for? Why slaughter a sweet little calf? And if it really was made to be slaughtered, why was it made so pretty? Wouldn't it have been enough if it had been born just a piece of meat inside a leather bag? Why does your mother want to kill it? Who gave her the right to kill such a pretty calf?"

I vowed that night to give eighteen pennies to the alms box of Rabbi Meir Baal Haness if only he would make my mother change her mind. Then I fell asleep.

In my dreams I saw a bound calf, over which stood the slaughterer, knife in hand. Down it came . . . the calf went into convulsions, the blood spurted out. . . .

When I rose from bed in the morning, I ran straight to the barn to discover to my relief that my darling calf was alive and well and peacefully resting. Its mother stood lovingly over it, licking its back with her tongue and arranging its short hairs in rows.

When I came home the next evening, I found the slaughterer talking figures with my mother and fixing a price for the calf's hide. I said nothing, because I had already been told that I was a fool, but my temper flared and my heart beat like a gong. Was I really such a fool, I wondered? But why? Who said that I musn't have pity on the pretty calf? My mother? But I'd heard her say more than once that we were commanded to be merciful to animals and not treat them cruelly! Not treat them cruelly—but slaughter them? Be merciful—and slaughter them? So she said, but who said she was right? Could she be wrong, then? Could mothers be wrong too? Dear God, my mother and the calf are both in Your hands —why did You make the calf live and make my mother want to kill it? God! Why should this calf, which You created perfect in all its parts so that it should be able to live for years on the face of Your earth, have to be slaughtered? If You knew in advance, God, which calves were meant to be slaughtered and which were not, why did You create the ones meant for slaughter and give them the power to live and to bring more life into the world after them? And if You made them to live, why should you be disobeyed? And what about my little brother who died when he was eight days old? My mother said that even before he was a twinkle in her eye it was written down in a book in heaven how long he would live—but then why was he born with all the makings of a man? What did he need legs for if he wasn't going to walk on them? What did he need hands for if he wasn't going to use them? And what about his mouth? And his lips? What would have happened if the wet nurse hadn't choked him accidentally? And why should she be blamed if it was really the Angel of Death's fault? My mother told me that it was, but if it was the wet nurse who choked the baby, what was there left for the Angel of Death to do? Was it possible for someone, even a little child, to die without him?

"Mama, can someone die without the Angel of Death?"

"Are you out of your mind, Hofni?" my mother exclaimed in embarrassment before the slaughterer, who broke into a broad smile at my idiotic question. "What's gotten into you? Do you already know the whole Talmud that you have nothing better to do than to worry about how people die?"

I was left feeling furious and crushed.

I couldn't sleep that night. Bitter, horrendous thoughts kept crossing my mind. I hid my face in the blanket because they frightened me so terribly and made me ask such tormenting questions. I felt as if some structure inside of me were collapsing, as if something were being torn from its place and uprooted. . . . I felt that I was at war—with myself, or rather that my mind was at war with my heart, which was in full retreat. Now it made one last stand against the mind's assaults . . . it stumbled and was downed. . . . I felt wounded to the core. . . .

I vowed eighteen more pennies to the alms box. "O God," I whispered the words of the night prayer intently and contritely like a penitent alone with his sinful heart, "into Thy hand I commit my spirit"— and I slept.

"Minute follows minute, day pursues day." The second day came and went, the third day, the fourth day, the fifth. . . . On the eighth day the calf would be killed. I went about in a daze.

The calf grew by leaps and bounds and skipped on its long, thin legs. It came running toward me whenever it saw me in the distance, prancing with giddy glee. I greeted it with an inaudible groan, laughing and crying at once.

The terrible eighth day arrived.

I watched the hideous moment come closer. The hours flew by. The sun climbed higher and higher . . . now it was already dipping to the west. How awful it was!

I knew that the calf would not, could not be slaughtered, yet my heart pounded within me. I knew that God would think of something . . . the angels would come to its rescue . . . the knife would explode or its throat turn to marble . . . there was no other way out. My mother was adamant—but a miracle was bound to take place. It was the only solution. The calf was so pretty, and I had promised so much to the alms box. All day long I'd kept raising the sum.

And yet—who knew?

My heart pounded. There were tears in my eyes. I was bursting with emotion. My thoughts raced out of control. It was too much to make sense of. Even the rabbi wouldn't know . . . no, I wouldn't even ask him. He would just laugh at me like my mother and call me a fool. . . .

They slaughtered the calf.

In the Evening

"Bring a candle back with you," the rabbi told me as I started home for lunch, "because as of to-night"—it was already autumn, the Sunday of the third Torah reading in the Book of Genesis—"all the boys studying Bible will remain in the evening as well. From now on each boy in the Bible class will have to bring a candle every week to light his place at the table. And you'll have to bring lanterns too, to light your way home at night."

Tonight I would begin to study in the evening, I thought as I walked home for lunch. What wonderful news! As soon as I reached home I would tell my

mother that I was now grown up. And I would tell my
sisters Breyndl and Sarka that I was too old to play
with them and their toys anymore. How splendid it
felt to be grown up! Just a year ago, I remembered,
I had still been considered a baby. "Hofni's too little,"
all the boys had said then, "he won't be studying
evenings." And the rabbi's assistant had had to carry
me home on his shoulders and tell my mother: "Hofni's still a little boy and can't wade through the mud
by himself." "Too little," "too little"—I was forever
hearing those words. How terribly I wanted to be
big, to study Bible and spend evenings in the heder.
My mother wanted me to grow up too. "How long
will this go on?" I once heard her ask the rabbi. "The
years fly by like shadows—is he to be allowed to grow
up wild like a shepherd or a swineherd?" "Hofni's
still too little," the rabbi had answered, "and isn't
ready to study Bible yet." Whereas now . . . now I
would be studying it, and in the evening too. How
splendid, how marvelous it felt!

I returned to the heder.
The mud in the streets seemed neck-high.
Beneath an overcast sky, the wind whipped thin
drops of rain that beat furiously against the pass-
ersby, who walked bent beneath the sufferance of
their torn, ragged cloaks, which were soaked through
with rain and grime. Boots struggled to break free of
the stubborn slush. An excruciating curtain of gloom,
the shadow of deep anxiety, lay over each despairing
face, though the one thing all felt was neither joy nor
sorrow but the single-minded desire to get through
the mud as quickly as possible to the safety of some

low, damp, dark home. I, Hofni, loved to stand at
such times on a bench by the window of the heder
and look out; I loved to watch the spray and the
pockmarks that formed on the surface of the puddles
when the rain spattered down on them; I loved to
look at the doleful faces of the people as they fought
their best with the flagstones and planks of wood that
had been strewn about to make footpaths, colliding
with each other when they met, grappling and losing
their balance until one or both of them fell. Mire and
muck, figures in silhouette, houses like sepulchers,
wet stone, bits of broken glass, snow and rain mixed
together . . . all were engraved on my heart in a grim
and terrible hand. I stood stock still and stared
straight ahead. There was nothing that I wanted,
nothing that I felt, nothing else that mattered in the
whole world. . . .

Dusk. The traffic in the street quickened slightly.
Little children were escorted home from the heder.
Men set out for the afternoon and evening prayer.
Women went to buy kerosene and other provisions.
Here and there a shopkeeper started for home, her
keys and bundles in one hand and a bucket of smol-
dering coals in the other. A dense fog filled the air.
It was getting darker. All I could make out from the
window were the shadows passing slowly through
the mist. The rabbi had gone off to pray. The rabbi's
wife was out buying kerosene and chatting with her
friends. The rabbi's assistants were taking the little
children home. The darkness outside had thickened
into a terrible gloom. The shadows vanished. I
turned from the window and faced the room, which
was dark and hushed. The boys stood in a circle and

huddled closely together. My flesh crept, my hair stood on end. Afraid to remain by the window alone, I joined the circle of boys.

One of them stood in the center and told in a low, woebegone voice of a youth who had awakened in the middle of the night to find that he had been sleeping in the Great Synagogue. The flame of the eternal light burning above the podium threw the building into dim relief. Suddenly the synagogue was filled with a great radiance and a loud commotion could be heard in the distance. It came nearer and nearer . . . Lord God of Hosts! The building was filling up with ghosts from end to end . . . they stood in white shrouds and swayed back and forth in prayer . . . they stepped up to the holy ark, took out the Torah scrolls, and the reader called out: "Let a priest come forth for the first blessing!"—and up to the Torah came a dead man wrapped in his prayer shawl and recited the blessing. "Let a Levite come forth for the second blessing!" called the reader, and a second ghost stepped up to the Torah. "Let a worshiper come forth for the third blessing!" called the reader. "Let a worshiper come forth for the fourth blessing!" And after all seven blessings had been said: "Let the groom Zerach the son of Reb Gronim come forth for the maftir!" The young man lay on the bench like a log, too petrified to stir or even blink. Whereupon the reader called out again: "Let the groom Zerach the son of Reb Gronim come forth for the maftir!" The young man hid his face in his hands but the voice called out once more: "Let the groom Zerach the son of Reb Gronim come forth for the maftir!" He fainted dead away . . . two ghosts were standing over him

. . . they carried him to the podium and stood him in front of the Torah scroll. "Say the blessing over the Torah!" thundered the ghost reader. He said the blessing and the ghost read the final portion. Then he himself read the portion from the Prophets together with all the ghosts and recited the blessings at the end of it while the dead men cried: "Amen!" The service was still in progress when the sexton of the Great Synagogue arrived to prepare for a midnight vigil. He rapped three times on the door—and immediately the great light went out and the ghosts disappeared, leaving the flame of the eternal light burning dimly again in the dark, shadowy building. The sexton found the youth in a swoon on the floor, from which he recovered long enough to tell what had happened—and then passed away.

The teller was done with his tale. The other boys stood with their mouths wide open, ready to listen endlessly on and on. In our fright, we had narrowed the circle even more. We held on to each other and pressed tightly together, prepared to defend one another against the ghost or the demon who might come to carry one of us off.

But there were more stories still to come. No sooner had one boy begun to tell about "the twelve thieves" than another interrupted him with "the king of the demons." The inventions multiplied, each of us seeking to outdo his neighbor with one that he knew . . . when suddenly the rabbi's wife appeared and lit the lamp. The room was flooded with light and we stood rubbing our eyes in the sudden glare. Our fears and fantasies took flight, our tall tales and thoughts were forgotten. For a moment we stood immobile, struck dumb as golems without mind or will. The rabbi and his assistants returned to the heder. A new din arose. The boys broke up and spread all over the room, some quarreling or conversing, others feasting on a crust of bread spread with a bit of herring, butter, cheese, chicken fat, or some other leftover from lunch.

The rabbi took his seat at the head of the table flanked by his two assistants, a leather-thonged switch placed before him. The children sat around the table on benches. The rabbi's voice mingled with the voices of his assistants and his young pupils. The noise was terrific. The switch lashed out, striking a child who burst into tears. But it did not return to the table. The rabbi's hand stayed outspread, his face contorted and a terrible wrath in his eyes. He was furious with the children, with his assistants, with his wife, with the table, with the switch, with the will of God for having created such a horrible, contentious world. In practically no time two children were crying, three children, four children, five. . . . The rabbi dealt out blows, shouted, and taught us the Bible on one side of the table, while his assistants did the same on the other. The third reading from the Book of Genesis flowed forth in a frightful lament, each word dripping with misery and the dread fear of God: "Get thee from thy land, and from thy kindred, and from thy father's house, to the land that I will show thee" . . . How terrible to have to get up now! It was fearfully dark outside. Rain, snow, and slush. The air was cold and damp. The fierce wind would slice through the holes of one's coat. At home were a mother and sisters, perhaps potatoes were baking there too—but even the rabbi and his switch seemed a pleasanter prospect than to have to venture outside by oneself.

One group of boys was dismissed by the rabbi and withdrew to the end of the bench while another took its place in front. There were more beatings and blows, loud shouts and cries, and the sorrowful, sob-watered chant: "Get thee from thy land, and from thy kindred, and from thy father's house, to the land that I will show thee" . . . The tumult began to die down. The rabbi was exhausted. His assistants belched and yawned. Several of the children were already nodding with their heads on their arms. The rabbi's wife sat darning a sock by the stove. The entire heder was filled with a toilsome, wearisome, enervating apathy. The one thing that we desperately wanted was to be allowed to go home at once. The desire grew stronger and stronger. It was all anyone thought about. We counted the minutes and scrutinized the rabbi's face to decipher from its grimaces whether he meant to let us go soon or not.

All at once he rose from the table with his assistants. There was a sudden scramble. The children jostled each other behind the table, battling to be first off the bench, eyes sparkling brightly with exuberance. Were it not for our fear of the rabbi, we would have danced deliriously in the aisles. Our young hearts felt a burst of wistful, mutual love, and we looked at each other with kind affection. All day long we had been cooped up together under the rabbi's horrible gaze, while now that it was averted and we were free at last, we had to bid one another good-bye and go each his own way. . . .

The assistants helped the children to button

their coats, wrapped thick scarves around their throats, straightened their caps, brushed back their earlocks, and sent them off in groups by the streets on which they lived. The rabbi cast a glance at us as he leaned against the table, but his magical power was broken. He could stand there as long as he pleased with his eyes hard upon us—the spell was gone from them and a dreadful fatigue had taken its place. His drawn face, which he now turned toward his wife, announced that in a moment he would scratch himself front and back and mumble drowsily: "Tsipa, let me have my dinner! I'm tired, I need to sleep."

We lit our lanterns and rushed noisily outside, bursting with youthful energy that demanded an outlet after its imprisonment throughout the long day. Our boyish hearts craved a moment of life. Forgotten were the heder with its sorcerers and demons, the rabbi with his cries of "bandits!" and "goyim!," his warnings of hellfire and the Angel of Death. For a minute each of us scampered gaily off by himself. It was terribly dark, and the cold cut through to the bone. A wettish stuff, indistinguishable in the night air as either rain or snow, struck wickedly at our faces and frozen ears and trickled now and then down our necks, from where it slithered to our chests and down again. Our feet fought desperately to keep their footing . . . but what did any of it matter when we were beside ourselves with joy? We chattered merrily, pushing each other in fun from the pathway into the mud and quarreling with spirited good humor.

Our ranks began to thin out. Every few minutes

another boy left the column with a loud cheer and disappeared into his home. The merriment died down. Our laughter trailed away. I was left by myself in the street. The wind wailed through the awful black stillness. Faint rays of light crept through the low windows to cast a mournful glance at the dead street. My lantern lit only a few square feet around me, making the darkness seem even thicker. I, Hofni, made my way in the dead of night through the perilous world, which was teeming with ghosts, demons, phantoms, sorcerers, and gypsies. . . . I was all alone . . . but I would be brave! I marched with giant steps . . . on I strode, utterly at the mercy of whoever might come along . . . one more narrow street . . . five more houses . . . four . . . three . . . ahead was my father's house . . . a light shone in the window! How good to be indoors where there were no ghosts to fear, no cold, no mud, no slippery paths—in a second I would be there! In I burst with a triumphant whoop, my lantern in one hand while I shut the door behind me with the other, and shouted heartily "good evening!" feeling every inch the grown man. My mother was sewing on a stool by the warm stove, mending her linen. A kerosene lamp burned dimly on the table in front of her. By the stool near the table hung a wicker crib, which she rocked back and forth with her foot by the rope which held it. She was putting my little brother, Sandrel, to sleep. My eldest sister, Breyndl, sat beside her on a wooden bench and practiced darning socks, while my youngest sister, Sarka, lay dozing on her lap. The beds were already made. There wasn't a sound in the room. My mother looked happy to see me. She didn't say a word, but I could tell by her face that she had been waiting for me impatiently. She threw me a sharp, probing glance as I came through the door.

"Are you all right, Hofni? What did you learn today in the heder, son? But Hofni, you must be hungry, aren't you?"

"Yes, mama, I'm starving."

"Here, let me give you a slice of bread with chicken fat."

"But, mama, I don't like chicken fat."

"Then have your bread with some pears."

"I don't want pears."

"Is it food fit for a king that you're asking for then, or is it the troubles of my soul?"

And she added angrily:

"That's what I get for spoiling you! Do you really think you're still an only child? There's Sandrel too, may he live, and Breyndl and Sarka also."

"But, mama, if you'll tell me a nice story I'll eat my bread with chicken fat."

My sister Breyndl looked at my mother with big eyes, as though begging her to agree. With a laugh both yielding and vexed, my mother said:

"Well then, I'll tell you a story about an unlucky boy, so that you'll know how fortunate you are to have a rabbi and a heder, and a father and a mother, and chicken fat and pears. Because this poor boy—"

"Mama," I interrupted her, "where's papa?"

"Your papa?" she asked with a sigh. "Your papa has gone to the fair . . . and on a rainy night like this! But perhaps he'll earn something there."

"But, mama," I said after a moment's silence, "tell us. Tell us the story!"

My mother put down her linens and bent to look at my sleeping brother, Sandrel. Then she pressed my sister Sarka to her breast and began:

"Long, long ago, when my grandmother's father was still a tiny little boy, and his parents lived in a village that belonged to a rich Polish landowner—so I heard from my grandmother when I myself was a little girl no bigger than you, Breyndl'e, and she was an old, old woman—there lived in the same village another Jew whose name was Reb Yosef. He was a very pious and a very learned man, and he collected the landowner's taxes, though he himself was very, very poor. The landowner was fond of him and used to call for him often to sing him Sabbath hymns and melodies from our holy days—the rich Christians too, Hofni my darling, like our melodies—and sometimes, when he was feeling merry with drink, he would ask him to dance for him. In return, he didn't press him for the tax money that he owed him. And so many, many years went by and Reb Yosef lived in peace and quiet. His wife—I can't remember her name—was a good-natured, hospitable, God-fearing woman. It was she who ran the tavern that they kept, while Reb Yosef spent most of his time shut up in his room, where he busied himself in study and in prayer. Even the Christians in the village knew that 'Yoske' was a holy man of God, and they honored him greatly for it. Now one day Reb Leib Sorehs, who was a disciple of the Baal Shem Tov, may his memory be blessed, happened to pass through the village and asked to spend the night at Reb Yosef's house. Reb Yosef and his wife had no idea that he was a holy man of God, but they gave him dinner and a place to sleep just as they did any guest. When morning came, Reb Leib Sorehs rose from his bed, prayed, and made ready to depart. 'I can't let you go,' Reb Yosef's wife said to him, 'until you've stayed and dined with us first.' She insisted—and he stayed. After the meal he reached for his satchel and his walking stick and, turning to Reb Yosef and his wife, said: 'It's clear from what I've seen that you're God-fearing folk and that the Good Lord's blessing is over this house. But tell me, good people, if there's anything you lack and any wish that I might ask for you. Perhaps the Lord will grant my request.' 'God be praised, we want for nothing,' Reb Yosef answered. 'We earn our living, meager and troublesome though it be, and we certainly don't wish for wealth. Why should we wish for it when we'd never know how to spend it? But there is one thing that we're missing'—Reb Yosef sighed as he spoke—'and that's a son to study Torah and grow wise. Daughters we have, thank the Lord, but what good are they to me? Come with me, dear guest, and I'll show you a bookcase full of books. Who will read them when I'm gone?' 'In that case, Reb Yosef,' said Reb Leib, 'when the year comes round again your wife will be cradling a son in her arms. The lad's soul will be a great one, great in Torah and in holiness, but Samael will set his eye on him, so that holiness will wrestle with the *klipa*' "—(we children already knew all these words, because my mother had told us such stories many a time)—"' and the struggle will be very, very bitter. Take heed then that you guard the boy well and keep him from anything unclean.' As soon as he finished speaking these words, he quickly opened the door and vanished away.

"Nine months passed and a boy was born to Reb

Yosef, as handsome as an angel of God. When the landowner heard the news, he sent for Reb Yosef and said to him: 'Listen here, Moshke'—that's what the landowner called him—'I hear, you poor man, that you've gotten yourself a son. What can you possibly want with a son, Moshke? Isn't it enough that you've brought so many daughters screaming into this world to grow up without a penny to their name? You might care to remember, Moshke, that you haven't paid me any taxes for the past eight years, which I've been kind enough to overlook. And what will this son of yours be? A Moshke like yourself! He'll wear your miserable clothes, and speak your miserable tongue, and sing your miserable songs in front of a landowner like myself. What kind of life will that be? Poverty and degradation, penury and deprivation, just like your own. Now I, Moshke, out of the goodness of my heart, feel compassion for the lad—who they tell me is a handsome child too—and I don't wish him to grow up an accursed, disgusting Jew. Give him over to me, Moshke, and let me raise him. I swear to you, he'll have the best of everything. I'm a lonely, childless man, and whatever riches God has granted me will be his too.'

" 'But your grace!' said Reb Yosef in a fright. 'You know that I'm a Jew. . . .'

" 'To hell with your Jewishness, you scum! A miserable Jew doesn't want a Polish nobleman to bring up his child! I'm giving you eight days to pay me my back taxes from the past eight years, and if you don't bring me the money, I'll have you and your wife and your children thrown into the pit in my yard. Do I make myself clear, Moshke?'

"Now this landowner was a great and terrible

sorcerer, so that when Reb Yosef told his wife what he had threatened, she said to him: 'Listen to me, husband. I've been told that the Baal Shem Tov, who is a man of God and can work miracles, is staying in a town not far from here. Go to him and ask him to give you a charm to protect the child against sorcery.' So Reb Yosef set out for the Baal Shem, and as soon as he entered the house where the Baal Shem was staying, he saw the old man whose blessing had brought him a son. Reb Yosef recognized him, but the old man pretended not to know him, until the Baal Shem called out: 'Leib! Why are you pretending? Let the world know that your powers are great in heaven and on earth! Go with this man and help him, be quick and don't fear. Take my stick with you too, but don't let go of it for a moment—remember that I've warned you. And take eight men along with you, so that you'll have a minyan for prayer. On the eve of the child's circumcision you're to stay up all night studying the Mishnah and reading in the *Zohar*, and you're to close all the doors and plug all the holes in the windows and the chimney. If anyone knocks on the door, you're not to open it. If anyone calls you, you musn't answer. Even if he calls in my name, you musn't reply. Remember, I've warned you!'

"The night arrived. The minyan assembled in the mother's room. Reb Leib Sorehs pronounced spells and incantations and drew a circle around the mother's bed with the Baal Shem's walking stick. He whispered holy names over it and said, turning to those present: 'You had better know now that the battle we must fight tonight will be very hard and grueling. Samael has summoned his forces because he wants to steal the child's soul; the landowner is a spark of Samael: he wants to take the child and raise him to be a goy, to hand him over to the *klipa*, God forbid. So brothers, be strong! Stay awake through the night studying the Mishnah and reading in the *Zohar* and don't take your eyes off your books for a second. You'll see and hear many things tonight, but you needn't be afraid. This stick'—and he raised it for all to see—'belongs to the Baal Shem, and it will drive away all goblins, wizards, and devils. So in the name of the Lord God of Israel, and of our master Israel ben Havah the Baal Shem Tov, don't be afraid! The Lord will fight for you, and ye shall hold your peace!'

"The words were scarcely out of his mouth when there came a loud knock on the door: 'Open up! In the name of the landowner, open up!' But no one opened. 'Open up! I'm the landowner's servant! He'll make you pay for it dearly, you miserable Jews, if you don't open the door!' But no one opened. Silence. . . . An hour went by and there was a knock on the door again: 'Open up! Moshke, open the door! It's I, the landowner. Moshke, don't you know who I am? Open up! I'll have you flogged with a wet birch rod tomorrow if you don't open up! Moshke! Moshke, I have something to tell you. Open the door! I'll have you thrown out for good tomorrow if you don't open up!' But no one opened. . . . Another hour went by and a great commotion could be heard far away. The noise was of a large crowd of men loudly approaching the house. Someone knocked rowdily on the door: 'Yoske, open the door, we want some brandy!' But no one opened. 'Yoske! What's the matter with you,

Yoske, why don't you open the door? We need a drink. Give us some brandy or we'll break the door down! Yoske, open up! Enjoy yourself all you want with your Jew friends from town, but give us our brandy. Give us brandy, Yoske, or we'll bash down the walls of your house until there isn't a stone left in place.' They banged furiously on the door until it seemed certain to break; they ripped the shutters from the windows and hurled through rocks; the house groaned out loud as though it were about to collapse on them all—but still no one opened. . . .

"Yet another hour passed and the distant sound of music could be heard. Ah, what a wonderful melody! It tugged hard at their legs to run greet the musicians. All their senses felt drugged: their hearts pounded, their eyes grew moist, their legs began to twitch of their own accord, the blood pulsed sweetly yet strangely through their veins in time to the music. The melody came nearer; they sought to stay in their seats and read on in the *Zohar*, but it kept calling them away. They mustered all their strength to stay put, but the music kept calling . . . their vision dimmed, thousands of dots swam helter-skelter before them . . . their eyelids craved sleep, their drowsy minds rest, but their hearts leaped within them for life—soon they would splinter into pieces from so much desire. . . . The sound came still closer. The music seemed to be directly behind the windows and door. Now it was sad, and their eyes filled with tears as they read in the *Zohar;* now it grew merry again, and they laughed as they read with sheer joy while their feet danced in place. The instruments called them. Their hearts were filled with a pleasant yearning. If only they could step out for a second and see the marvelous musicians—but it was forbidden. Reb Leib stood leaning on the walking stick with all his might, his lips moving soundlessly through charms and incantations. The music stopped . . . suddenly there was a knock on the door: 'Open in the name of Rabbi Israel Baal Shem!' 'Coming!' called out one of the minyan. Reb Leib shuddered and made a face . . . but it was already too late: a black cat sprang into the house, ran to the bed, snatched the child from its mother, and disappeared. 'Samael has triumphed!' Reb Leib exclaimed and fell unconscious to the floor.

"The next morning Reb Yosef came to the manor house and asked to be admitted by the servants to see the landowner.

" 'The landowner's orders are to flog you fifty strokes with a wet birch rod,' the servants said.

" 'But in God's name,' Reb Yosef protested, 'what crime have I committed? Let him give me back my son and flog me eighty strokes! I beg you, for the love of God, let me see the landowner.'

" 'Beat him without mercy!' came the landowner's voice from within the house.

"Reb Yosef died the next day and his family was banished from the village.

"The boy grew up in the landowner's house. He was a striking, fair-eyed lad, bright and attentive, and the landowner loved him dearly. He taught him all seven sciences and was amazed at how quickly he learned.

" 'Father!' the boy asked one day. 'Tell me, what is a *zhid?*'

" 'A *zhid* is an evil spirit, a devil, an imp.'

" 'Then why do all the boys in the manor yard call me a *zhid?*'

" 'I wouldn't know,' said the landowner, biting his lips in anger.

"From that day on he wasn't called *zhid* any more.

" 'Father!' he asked another time. 'I saw you talking today to a miserable, stooped-looking man, and you said to him, 'Moshke, you dog.' And as he was leaving the boys called him *zhid* and threw rocks at him. Is he really a devil? Aren't you afraid of him?'

" 'No, my son, he's a Jew, a member of that miserable, damned race on which the curse of God rests eternally.'

" 'But are a Jew and a devil the same?'

" 'Exactly the same, son.'

" 'Father!' the boy asked yet another time when he was twelve years old. 'Am I really a *zhid?* Today one of the boys in the yard said to me: 'Peter, you may as well know you're a *zhid*. My father told me last night that your father was a *zhid* and that his name was Yoske. My father said that your father was a good, honest man, and that he never got drunk or beat his wife, but that he prayed all day long to the God of the *zhids.*' Is it true, father, that I'm really a *zhid?*'

" 'No, son, it's a lie!' the landowner answered distraughtly.

"But before the boy's thirteenth birthday he dreamt a dream in which a white-haired old man was standing over him. His face was all bruised and looked poor and ill-favored like a sick *zhid's*. 'I'm

your father,' the bowed old man exclaimed. 'The
landowner snatched you from your mother's lap, and
me, your father, he killed. But you're a Jew and you
must live like a Jew. . . . In a few days' time you'll be
thirteen years old, and a Jewish boy of thirteen is
commanded to perform God's will and to devote
himself to His holy Torah. Come, rise, my son, and
follow me.'

"The boy shuddered and cried out in his sleep—
and awoke.

" 'What made you cry last night?' the landowner
asked him when he rose the next morning.

" 'I had a terrible dream, father!' answered the
boy with tears in his eyes.

" 'What was it, son? Tell me about it. Dreams
mustn't be taken seriously.'

" 'Oh, father, I'm afraid even to tell you . . . it's
so awful . . . in my dream a flayed, beaten *zhid* came
up to me, and he said he was my father, and that I
was a Jew, and he said that I must follow him. Ah,
father, is it really true that I'm a *zhid*? The boys in
the yard say I'm one too.'

" 'They're lying,' said the landowner, 'and your
dream doesn't mean a thing.' But it was clear to see
that he was frantic.

" 'Oh, father!' said the boy the next morning.
'Last night the Jew beat me terribly. He pulled my
hair and scratched me with his nails until I bled. If
only you could have seen how awful he looked with
his bloodshot eyes and his wrinkled brow, which
seemed so full of worry and affliction . . . if only you
could have heard how dreadful he sounded when he
said to me: "You're a Jew and I'm your father: rise

and follow me, or else I'll kill you right now!" . . . if only . . . oh, father, father, father!'

"And on the third morning, when he awoke from his sleep, he found himself lying naked in one of the streets of the village on the threshhold of the synagogue.

"That night the rabbi of the village dreamt that he saw a white-haired old man with an angel's face and a voice as soft and sweet as a lute, in which he implored him: 'Rabbi, tomorrow morning, on the threshold of the synagogue, the sextons will find a naked, handsome, fair-eyed boy. The boy is my son. The landowner made off with him by black magic, murdered me, and banished my wife and children from the village. Tomorrow the boy will be thirteen years old, yet he doesn't know a word of Yiddish or a letter of the Hebrew alphabet. I beg you, be a father to him; teach him God's Torah and the way of His commandments. And know too that his is a great soul, but that Samael lies always in wait for it, so that you must wage the Lord's battle to keep the fiend from carrying it off through your gates.'

"The rabbi took the boy into his home.

"By the end of the first day the boy had learned the letters of the alphabet. By the second he knew the vowels too. By the third he could read in the prayer book. By the fourth he was able to pray. By the fifth he began to study Bible. The rabbi loved him like a father and the rabbi's wife raised him as though he were her own. Whatever he did, he did well, and all were amazed at his prowess in Torah.

" 'My boy!' the rabbi said to him one morning. 'You were born to be a great rabbi and scholar in

Israel, and I can no longer be your teacher. Here, take this letter of recommendation to Amsterdam, where you'll study in the Great Yeshivah. But always remember your dead father, and remember me too, and the God of Israel, who is One. Never forget, my boy, that Satan lies in wait for your soul. Both your father and I have fought mightily to save it, but now it is God's will that you leave me, for it's time you were put to the test. Here, take this amulet, and take my walking stick too, which I shall give you. Whenever you lie down to sleep, make a circle around you with this stick, and don't dare leave it until sunup. And hold this amulet in your hand until you rise. Remember, I've warned you! Now be of good cheer.'

"Then the rabbi fell upon the boy's neck and wept, and the boy wept too, and the rabbi's wife wept too where she stood.

"The boy shouldered his pack—and set out.

"And so the young lad, who had been raised in satins and silks, whose every step had been guarded like the apple of their eye by valets, tutors, governesses, menservants, and maidservants, now made his way on foot with a pack on his back. The way was a long one. He had to pass towns and villages, rivers and forests, in order to reach the Great Yeshivah in Amsterdam. But pass them he must, and he did. His path took him through a great forest. Huge oak trees towered by each side of the road. The way seemed endless, the forest too seemed endlessly deep. The sun began to set. His feet were weary from walking. He stopped to recite the afternoon prayer while darkness covered the earth, and then he recited the evening prayer too. After he had prayed he took a crust of bread from his pack and sat down to eat. But there was no water with which to wash his hands. How could he eat without washing? He felt terribly tired and weak. His eyes began to close on their own. He said the *Shema* and drew a circle around where he lay. Then, clutching the amulet in his hand, he placed the pack beneath his head and fell asleep.

"He had hardly shut his eyes when a great noise awoke him. When he opened them, he spied a pack of wolves racing through the forest and heading straight for him. The wolves' eyes glittered like fire and their horrible, sharp fangs were bared in their gaping mouths. The pack came nearer and nearer . . . it reached the limits of the circle . . . it pressed against them to cross them, but it couldn't break through. The harder the wolves tried, the harder they were thrown back, so that they danced insanely with fury. But they couldn't cross the circle. The wolves vanished . . . and out of the forest rushed a wild boar. It charged as far as the circle and halted, because it couldn't advance any farther. Then the boar vanished too, and all of a sudden the most wonderful music came forth from the depths of the forest. It was wafted on the wings of the unsullied wind which was then blowing softly through the forest, and which blew all the way from the Garden of Eden at the stroke of midnight when the gates of paradise swung open for the thirty-six Just Souls who came every night to study Torah with the Seven Shepherds. He felt that the wonderful musicians were calling to him . . . he remembered the landowner and his fiddle . . . yes, the landowner was a marvelous fiddler, and he had taught the boy to fiddle too. How he had loved his little fiddle! He wanted to step out of the circle, but he forced himself not to. His heart melted within him from desire like water . . . his hands shook, the amulet slipped from his grasp . . . it fell to the ground, and against his will he was dragged from the circle and carried off on the wings of the wind, up and away after the sound of the music. He flew over oceans and rivers, fields and forests, while the musicians played before him. They seemed just a handbreadth away, but he couldn't catch up with them. Here was his native village . . . here was the landowner's house . . . he was standing in front of the door . . . it opened, and . . . and a powerful large hand seized him and jerked him back. There was a furious struggle. One force pulled him mightily into the landowner's house, while another pulled him just as mightily back. 'I'm your father,' called a figure like that he had seen in his dream. 'I'm Yosef your father and you're my son. Don't you recognize me? I'm your father, and you're my son. You're a Jew, you mustn't enter the house! Here you'll become a goy, a creature of appetite, a drunk! Don't follow the music of the fiddle. The music is the service of a strange god and the fiddler is Asmodai, Satan himself. Son, go to Amsterdam, to the yeshivah. There you'll study Torah, the Law of the living God! Look at me, son: my flesh is tattered and flayed; the cruel landowner flogged me. If you become a landowner, you'll be cruel too. Son, go to Amsterdam and study Torah! Don't listen to the music of the fiddle . . . here, take this amulet which you lost in the forest. Go back, my son, go back.' And once again he was carried off on the wings of the—"

My little brother, Sandrel, suddenly woke from his sleep and began to cry. My mother broke off her story and bent down to quiet him, then laid my sister Sarka on her bed. My sister Breyndl was drowsing sitting up, a stocking in one hand and her ball of yarn and darning needle in the other. Her eyes were shut and her head bobbed up and down, tossing her pretty curls to and fro. The oil was nearly gone from the lamp, whose light grew steadily dimmer. Patches of darkness spread over the room. The blackened ceiling cast its shadow halfway down the walls. A terrible melancholy filled the house. Something hung in the air and I didn't know what, whether it was good or evil, holy or unclean, but I did know that whatever it was, it was dreadful. Yes, the house was dreadful, the heder was dreadful, the rabbi was dreadful, the synagogue was dreadful, the world was dreadful, and life was dreadful . . . and in this dreadful life we had to battle every minute with dreadful powers that lay constantly in wait for us. We had to battle with the goyim, with imps disguised as chimney sweeps, with the unclean lizards who brought the fire with which to burn down the Temple of our Lord, with exile, with demons, with the Evil Urge. Sometimes the Evil Urge might even tempt a Jew to look at a woman or to eat unclean meat . . . ah, how dreadful it was! The Evil Urge was so strong! How hard it was to have to lead such a dreadful, sinful life! The tears came to my eyes. My mother looked at me and said:

"Hofni, tomorrow I'll tell you the rest. Now say the *Shema* and kiss the mezuzah and go to sleep, because there's no oil left in the lamp and this is no time for telling stories."

"But, mama, what happened to the boy in the end?"

"I'll tell you the rest tomorrow."

"But did he stay with the landowner?"

"No, it's still a long story. I'll tell you the rest tomorrow. The boy stayed a good Jew, and you too, Hofni, must be a good Jew like your forefathers."

Full of emotion I said the *Shema* and kissed the mezuzah. When I lay down in bed I continued to think fondly of the brave boy, who strove with Samael and prevailed, until my eyes shut tight and I slept.

The
Amulet

I woke up crying in the middle of the night.

"What is it, Hofni?" asked my mother, awakened too by the sound of my tears. "What are you crying for?"

"I'm scared, mama, I'm so scared. Please light the candle for me, please do."

"But why should you be scared, Hofni?" my mother asked in an unsteady voice. "Of what?" She quickly lit the kerosene lamp, trimming back the wick to keep it from burning too brightly.

"I'm so scared, mama. I had a dream, and when I woke I couldn't remember it. And now I've been

lying in bed for a whole hour and I can't sleep. It's so
scary to be up all alone in the middle of the night."
   "Don't be a silly thing," my mother said in a thin,
hoarse voice, and fell asleep again.
   I turned to stare directly at the dim lamp. The
silence that prevailed in the house was broken only
by the snoring of the sleepers, which sounded slowly
and in sequence like an orchestrated theme. The
lamp stood at one end of a table over most of which
it cast its light, throwing into relief the half-empty
water jug that had been set out for hands to be
washed before prayer in the morning. Farther on a
thick pall of darkness covered everything. The two
chairs by the table seemed awfully ominous and
black; the light made its way up through the house
from the lamp to the ceiling, where it played back
and forth harmonically, dancing and jigging before
yielding to the pitch-black darkness beyond it, which
had a shape and form of its own and seemed terribly
thick, black, and crude. The black half-jug was like a
monstrous apparition. I turned to stare again at my
mother's bed, but all I could make out was the side-
board and the corner of her pillow. My mind was a
perfect blank. I lay without stirring, unconscious of
whether I was awake or asleep.... Gradually, I began
to think again—yet not to think either, but to
precariously feel, as though a sound like a bell had
rung in my ear and restored me to my senses, so that
I remembered that I was awake, and began dimly
and disconnectedly to associate: the lamp, the wick,
the light, and on and on ... and all kinds of other just
as vague things and sensations, or so it seemed: demons, ghosts, my father, the rabbi, the fair ... and

still other things too that I couldn't name. Something was terribly wrong—but what? I couldn't sleep—but why not? And where was my mother? I wasn't in a magic circle in the forest or in the Great Synagogue . . . I could feel the pillow beneath me . . . yes, I was lying on it. I wanted to cry, but it would make my mother angry. I decided to say the *Shema.* My mother had once told me that whenever she was frightened at night she said the *Shema.* But my hands were unclean for prayer. I could have leaned over to the water jug and washed them, I even wanted to, but I couldn't. My will was too weak to make me obey it. I couldn't even take my hands out from under the covers. I wanted to wake my mother, but I was afraid to make a sound. . . .

It was an awful, an intolerable situation. Without realizing it, I had begun to cry again, at first at intervals and in an almost inaudible whisper, alternately releasing a sob and stopping to listen to it and contemplate the way it calmed and revived me: I was not, after all, alone by myself; there was this other thing beside me. My own voice was a sign of life, and where there was life, fear vanished. My sobs proceeded as though by themselves in short, low bursts that periodically grew longer and louder in progression. . . .

"Hofni, what is it?" my mother called out in distress, waking again from her sleep. "Why are you crying, Hofni?"

The sound of her voice immediately broke the bad spell and brought me back to myself.

"What *is* the matter, Hofni?" she asked again anxiously, when I awoke a second night crying once more. "What is it, son? What are you crying for this time?"

"Oh, mama, I'm so afraid! I saw the old holy man in my dream, the one grandmother told me about. Oh, mama, let me into bed with you and I'll tell you all about it. . . . Don't you remember the old holy man that grandmother told us about? She said that he was my grandfather, I mean my great-grandfather, and that he lived in Polonnoye in Chmielnicki's time— didn't you also tell me all about Chmielnicki and the holy man?—and now I saw him in my dream, and he went dressed in white shrouds to Chmielnicki's army, and he said: 'Go ahead and kill me, I surrender my soul to be a martyr of God! Hear, O Israel, the Lord our God, the Lord is one!' And then they killed him. . . . Ah, mama, are there still holy men now too? Does the blood still come up to your knees in Polonnoye? And why aren't there holy men in our village too? My friend Shlumiel told me that in Chmielnicki's time the boys didn't study in the heder. But once Chmielnicki came to a heder, and he found it full of boys, and the rabbi and his assistants were teaching them to read, and the rabbi said to them: 'Don't be afraid, children, we're leaving this filthy, con- taminated world to these cossacks, and we, in the name of our God, are going to paradise, to the holy fathers Abraham, Isaac, and Jacob.' And while Chmielnicki was slaughtering the children, the rabbi said the *Shema* with them, and he said it very loud so that all the mothers came too, and the cossacks killed them too, and they poured their blood on the babies. And then the fathers came too, and they killed them too, and they poured the blood on the mothers. And then—Shlumiel told me all this—all the blood was mixed together, the children's and the rabbi's and the assistants' and the rabbi's wife's and her children's and the mothers' and the fathers', and it flowed like a stream through the city streets until it came to the river, and it turned that red too. Oh, mama, mama, it's so awful!"

My mother bent over me and said, hugging me in her arms: "Don't be afraid, Hofni, don't. Tomorrow I'll have the old midwife come, and she'll rub you down with an egg so that you won't be afraid anymore."

"Zalman," said my mother to my father when he came home from the fair, "it's too much for me. For the past five nights Hofni has awakened with the most awful crying fits. The midwife rubbed him with an egg, and I even had the gypsy woman come, but he just cries and cries. During the day he wastes away in the heder, and when evening comes—the rabbi's assistant told me—he begins to tremble at his own shadow and sobs and screams. It's too much for me. What am I to do?"

"He's just being a foolish little boy!"

And turning to me, my father asked:

"What are you crying for, fool?"

"I'm afraid, papa. I'm afraid of the dark, and of the shadows too. . . ."

"If you were to listen to me, Zalman," my mother said, "I'd advise you to take him to the holy rabbi, may he live. I don't like it, and I have a feeling that it's nothing to make light of. Please, forget about your business and go with him to the rabbi. Do you hear me?"

"Forget about my business?" asked my father with bitter irony. "That's easy enough, there's little to forget in the first place. But where am I to get the money to pay for the journey and for the warm clothes to travel with in weather like this? I won't do it. You're just a woman; you don't know a thing and you can't. I have my reasons, but you won't and can't understand them . . . even if I had the money and the clothing, I wouldn't go. I have reasons that you can't understand! There's no one, no one for me to go to —do you understand me now? But of course you don't! How could you? I'm a man with an open wound in his heart—but what do you know about Hasidism? Even in the *klayzl* hardly anyone understands; even those who go to the rabbi don't understand . . . woe to evil days such as these!.The heart is covered with ashes! Heresy, free thought, superficiality, hard times, and exile—and all the while the flame is growing dimmer, the flame is going out. . . . The old rabbi Shneur Zalman is dead. What our Hasidic leaders used to understand in the old days, what I learned from my fathers, next to whom I'm not even like a dog lapping at the sea, our rabbi himself doesn't understand today. Don't look so astonished. You're a woman and you can't understand, but we're a shepherdless flock nowadays. We have no father, none. Do you hear me? We have no one to lean on but our Father in heaven. I'm not going. I won't . . ."

"I beg you," my mother pleaded, "don't sin before God with your talk. It's not for the likes of us to stick our heads between mountains."

"Let me be. You're a woman and you don't know a thing. I may be a poor, downtrodden, itinerant Jew, but a Jew I still am . . . and I know what a 'degree' is. I know what the degree of the Baal Shem Tov was, the degree of the Maggid of Mezritsh, the degree of the Grandfather of Shpola, the degree of the Old Man of Chernobyl. But you don't know what a degree is at all. You think of it in the ordinary sense of the word, but you've never understood the holy books—there are secrets that you can't begin to understand. I shouldn't even be talking about them to a woman. Even in the *klayzl* almost no one understands anymore—because you might as well know that a degree isn't simple. It's something very, very deep. I have my reasons that you can't understand . . . if only I could be sure that at least the rabbi knew what a degree was . . . but I doubt even that . . . wherever I look things are falling apart! All that our fathers built is falling apart! And my heart tells me that the worst is yet to come. Everything will be laid waste. All Judaism will be laid waste because of the sins of this generation. I don't know what will become of this son Hofni of ours. A man needs a point of connection—that's also something you can't understand—and the less holiness there is, the more he connects with the *klipa*. And there's no strong tree in sight, no tsaddik to protect us. . . . No, I won't go. I'd do better to take him to Shemaiah the Cabalist. True, he's not one of us; he's a misnagid who thinks that the great chain stopped with Rabbi Isaac Luria and Hayyim Vital, so that he denies that divine inspiration still exists and won't hear of the sacred line of descent from the Baal Shem Tov to the old rabbi Shneur Zalman—that's another secret you can't understand—but a little is still better than nothing. At

least he knows the meaning of a degree. . . . Yes, I'll
go to him and to no one else."

My mother washed my face, scrubbing my
mouth, teeth, and eyes, neatly curled my long earlocks, and helped me into my Sabbath suit, over
which she put my winter coat after cleaning it of the
layer of mud and dirt that clung to it from the autumn rains. Then she set my cap straight on my head
and said, after studying me for a moment and nodding with satisfaction:

"Now listen, Hofni, be a good boy. You're going
with your father to Rabbi Shemaiah the Cabalist, and
Rabbi Shemaiah is a great man, your father says, a
fine Jew, and a person of high degree. Master of the
Universe, one could wish that you grew up to be the
same! And really, Hofni, you could some day be like
him if you wanted. It would certainly be no disgrace
to your holy forefathers, of whom you wouldn't need
to feel ashamed even if you were greater than him.
Now run along and be a good boy, so that he needn't
be cross with you."

"Do you know where you're going?" my father
asked me as we stepped from the house.

"To Rabbi Shemaiah the Cabalist, papa."

"And who is Rabbi Shemaiah the Cabalist; do
you know?"

"Rabbi Shemaiah is a fine Jew, a great Jew.
That's what mama told me."

"And that's all? He's a Cabalist and a man of
degree besides! And why are you going to him,
Hofni?"

"Why? It must be because of what you told
mama."

"Ah, Hofni, if only you understood! Yes, I told your mama, but all she cares about is worldly things, earning a living and getting along in this life. That's why she's upset about your crying. She makes a big fuss over it, but I know that it doesn't mean a thing. You're just being a silly, foolish boy, that's why you cry. Really now, why should you cry? What do you see that's worth crying about? You don't have to worry about a living, and as for spiritual things, you're still too young for them. You certainly aren't crying because the Shekhinah is in exile! But because the opportunity presented itself, I'm taking you to Rabbi Shemaiah anyway. It's a good introduction to the study of Torah and the fear of heaven to see the face of an honest man, and men like Rabbi Shemaiah"—my father heaved a sigh—"are becoming scarcer all the time. Who knows whether in your generation they'll still be found at all. The times mock us to our faces. We can feel how this world is no longer our own, how our lives are no longer our lives, how everything has changed on account of our sins . . ."

My father didn't finish his thoughts because he had suddenly noticed that we were standing knee-deep in mud. Taking me in his arms, he rescued me from the quagmire and put me down on a wooden plank that lay by the side of the road. We worked our way along step by step, picking out a path among boards and bits of stone. More than once my father had to help me by picking me up and carrying me from one clear stretch to the next until we reached the Cabalist. The mud in his front yard was so deep that my father had to pick me up once more and

carry me across it. He opened the door and we found
ourselves standing in the cabalist's prayer room.

"Does the cabalist live here in the *klayzl*, papa?
I think this must be a *klayzl*, don't you?"

"It's his own private *klayzl*. But he has a house
too."

And addressing one of the occupants of the
room, my father asked:

"Is the cabalist at home?"

"He is."

My father opened a second door that led to the
house and we entered a long, dark hallway. He
opened another door and we entered a small room.
A rectangular table, painted red, stood several feet
from the window. A long bookshelf, across from
which were two wooden chairs, ran parallel to it.
Along one of the table's short sides stood a stool, and
opposite it, at the head of the table, a large chair, in
which sat a white-haired old man who was staring
intently at a large, thick book that lay on the wood
top before him.

My father made a noise, in order, I guessed, to
attract the old man's attention.

The cabalist looked up and let his glance roam
over each corner of the room before it came to rest
on my father and me. It frightened me terribly. Sunk
deep in their sockets, his large, dark eyes made me
think of burning coals; above their slit, guarded
pupils loomed a high, white forehead, furrowed up
and down with many wrinkles; his earlocks hung
down in dishevelment, his beard was long, his gaunt,
sallow cheeks had a bluish tincture like that of a
corpse. I was too petrified to look back. It was awe-

some, his gaze; his head seemed holy and majestic to me, though I couldn't have said why. My mind worked its way through a furious profusion of fantasies and thoughts, but all were left off in the middle, and the one thing I knew in the end, the only thing I felt, was that here was a different, a magical and holy world. The room was small and sparse; the Jew sitting in it was no less thin and haggard-looking than all Jews; but what a difference nonetheless! I could feel deep within me how utterly exalted he was, how much holiness and purity were in the air of his small room.

"Well, well, Zalman," the cabalist declared. "What brings you here, and who is the young man?"

"The young man is my son, rabbi. Boys will be boys. For the past several nights he's awakened from his sleep crying and screaming terribly. And during the day he wastes away in the heder like a melancholic."

The old man turned to stare at me, and I clutched in fear at the tails of my father's coat.

"Does he study in the heder?"

"Yes, rabbi, with Gad the melamed."

"Does he say the *Shema* every night?"

"He does."

"His *tsitsis* are in order?"

"They are."

"And the mezuzahs in your house too?"

"The mezuzahs too."

"It's nothing, nothing at all; he's a silly boy and he cries. But Zalman, if these little ones cry over nothing, how much is there for us grown men to cry over! Ah, Zalman, tell me, what will become of this son of yours? I'm not saying, God forbid, that you'll

expose him to the *klipa,* but I'm afraid—may the
devil stop his ears—that it may lure him in spite of
himself. Who knows what the future holds in store?
The Messiah hasn't come, there's nowhere left to
turn. Our generation has lost the power of expect-
ancy; we no longer have men of faith; the inner mind
has shrunk to nothing; the Shekhinah refuses to descend from her ten spheres. . . . Let me tell you a
deep truth, though it isn't easy to fathom: the fathers
who send their children to secular schools, the freethinkers who read forbidden books—none of them
have any choice, because holiness has departed this
world on account of our many sins. And because holiness has departed and left a vacuum behind, Samael
has spread his nets and goes forth to stalk souls. It's
as clear as day for whoever has eyes to see . . . holiness
is gone from the world . . . woe, woe, woe is us!" The
old man raised his voice in a wail. "We no longer
have a foothold in this world! There's no room for us
anymore! We're in exile together with the Shekhinah. . . ."

I didn't understand a word but the conversation
moved me deeply. I understood one thing: that the
situation was desperate, the battle fierce. The Evil
Urge was a hard opponent. He was an angel—a bad
one of course, but an angel nevertheless. Ah, I
thought to myself, what can this dreary, muddy, dirty
world be worth that we should have to fight for it and
suffer for it so much? Hadn't my mother once told me
that little babies had to be watched in their cribs so
that the demons didn't choke them at night? Even
little babies in their cribs had to fight for their lives!
And the struggle would go on forever, forever!

"Here's an amulet for you," said my father, in-

terrupting my thoughts. "The rabbi has given it to
you. Go to the rabbi and he'll tie it around your neck.
Go!"

He took my hand and let me to the cabalist.

The cabalist tied the amulet around my neck
and said in a trembling voice:

"Your name is Hofni? Be a good Jew, Hofni!"

"Amen!" answered my father. He took me by
the hand and we left.

I felt like a hero when we left. I was a soldier, I'd
been issued my arms—now the fight was up to me.

Whither?

Whither?

I see his melancholy profile as though through a mist, through the curtain of thick cloud that descended on him in his lifetime and darkened his bright trail with a multitude of vain fictions and will-o'-the-wisps—yes, I see him, poor devil, who thought so much about life and received nothing back in return, not even a decent remembrance when it was over.

Let this be his epitaph.

My mother told me many a story when I was a child, stories as dark and as dreadful as the darkness of the Exile and as ghastly and grim as the history of the Jews. My gray hairs and beard have nothing to do with old age, because I was already old as a boy; each of her stories bleached one more hair, until the color was gone from them all. I know now of course that there are persons on life's stage who eat, drink, and stay merry well enough . . . who aren't perpetually bowed beneath the curses of a vengeful God . . . yet then all of life presented itself to me as a terrible tragedy . . . and most terrible of all was the story of crazy Nachman, which we children discussed all the time in the heder, because we too knew all about it, down to its last eccentric detail.

"Reb Moshe, crazy Nachman's father," my mother once told me, "was a brilliant rabbi and a saintly Jew, but the old holy man of Chernobyl was even greater, and Reb Moshe didn't believe in him. Once the old man came to visit our town, but Reb Moshe refused to greet him, and when the old man sent for him specially, Reb Moshe wouldn't go. That Sabbath, when they were both in the synagogue, the old man turned to him and said: 'So you don't believe in me, Moshe? Let this be a sign to you. I know you've been wanting a son. This year your wife will give birth to one. There was once a great soul in the upper worlds, a very great and holy spirit, but Samael made off with it and ever since it's been in his clutches, hovering in the void for seventy years. I had thought I might rescue it from him, and so I've kept it from descending to earth, but now I see that the task is too much for me because of this sinful generation, which doesn't believe in me, so that my powers have been sapped. This soul will be—your son. He will be a great student of Torah and of wisdom, but all will go to Samael in the end, to the *klipa*. And because of him, you'll go down to your grave a broken old man.' "

"Crazy Nachman," our rabbi once told us in the heder when he was feeling well-disposed, "had great gifts of mind, but he couldn't resist the temptation to study cabala, even though he knew that it was forbidden under twenty-five years of age. He entered the mystic gardens and was struck down by what he saw, like Elisha ben Avuyah before him."

Crazy Nachman, went the story, was sitting over his books in the study house one night when suddenly he heard a horrid voice call out: "Nachman, I want a pinch of snuff!" When he looked up, he saw a long tongue sticking out at him from the women's gallery. . . . He took leave of his senses right then and there—and never came back to them.

"Crazy Nachman," a boy once told me, "wanted to know what's above and what's below, what's ahead and what's behind. He looked where he shouldn't have. Even now he goes on thinking the same weird thoughts. He doesn't think he's crazy at all."

The worst conflagration is that which flares up from the depths. All the water in the world can't extinguish such a fire before it has gutted everything in its way, because by the time it has been discovered, it is already burning full blaze and nothing can be snatched from its jaws. Such is the battle that a man fights within himself with his own heart and soul. It is the most dreadful battle of all, in which the heart is reduced to ruins long before the flame bursts into the open.

There was nothing really that sudden about Nachman's "madness" or about the sacrilege that he committed on that awful day.

The Day of Atonement. The synagogue was filled from wall to wall with men in white prayer gowns and prayer shawls. Reb Moshe stood by the ark in a tearful, prayerful study. His silvery beard hanging over his gown, his high, broad forehead, pale face, and deep-set black eyes, and the outlines of his back configured in white combined to give him an angelic appearance. On the podium in the center of the synagogue stood a frail, sickly young man with a white, cadaverous face and long, jutting jaws from the juncture of which grew a short, black beard. His large, dark eyes shone through their oval circuits like burning coals. The lines on his face and the expression in his eyes bore witness to the fact that here was someone who had thought much and deeply. At times his meditations were interrupted by the melodies of the cantor, which made him look up and stare oddly at his surroundings, as though he couldn't believe what he saw, or understand the meaning of it, or why he in particular should be among all these people on an evening like this. The crowd of worshipers regarded him with deference, for it knew that no ordinary thoughts could be passing through the head of Reb Nachman, the rabbi's son, the new star ascendant in Jewish skies. He was barely twenty years old—and already his fame had spread far and wide.

The service drew to an end. The cantor finished singing the "Song of Unity." Reb Nachman was still lost in thought, in deep contemplation of that marvelous philosophic poem that was so rich in life, faith, and intellectual inquiry, when a young Talmud student approached him with a question about the ritual performed by the high priest on this holiest of days in ancient times. The student addressed him once and yet again but received no answer. Amazed that the young man should be so involved with his thoughts as to be oblivious of what was said to him, the members of the congregation pressed closer. The student asked his question again. Suddenly Reb Nachman stirred and looked about with a strange and distracted glance. Turning on his questioner, he bitterly exclaimed:

"Ah! How long will this waste of life be allowed to go on?"

"What?" asked the bewildered student. "What waste of life do you mean?"

"You wouldn't understand," sighed Reb Nachman with a glance of his dark eyes.

The crowd of worshipers stared at him curiously. His father, the rabbi, came over too. Nachman's eyes burned like fire. He wanted to say something bitterer yet, something that had plagued him for days and for years and had been like salt in his wounds on this evening too, but to whom could he say it? Who was there to understand him and to follow his thought to the end? He stood leaning against the podium, from where he looked back at the congregation with a mixture of pity, anguish, and despair. Then he faced the young student again and went on:

"Yes, it's all nonsense. What does the high priest mean to you? Why should you care about something that happened thousands of years ago?"

"What's the matter with you, Nachman?" his father cried out. "Have you gone mad?"

"It's all nonsense!" he declared. And he picked up the candle that stood burning on the podium—and blew it out.

"He's gone mad!" his father cried harshly, and fell down in a daze.

The irreversible sentence was passed on the spot: he was "mad."

The members of the congregation stood whispering to each other with sad looks and strained voices, staring now at the elderly rabbi, who lay propped on his hands with his face to the floor as though ashamed to face the large crowd, now at his lunatic son, who had tarred himself in public with his own brush, and now at one another with upturned, unfathoming faces. It was too much to grasp. How could it have happened?

The lunatic remained leaning against a lectern, his face aflame, his eyes shooting strange sparks of fire as though he had really gone mad. He saw and felt in a flash how all had been ruined; he knew that in an instant's time he had hurled himself down an abyss and destroyed everything that he, and not only he, had labored to build in a lifetime. His good name, his good fortune, now lay at the bottom of these dizzying, dread depths. He saw the future stretch bleakly before him . . . now, at this very moment, he had already begun a new life—who knew or could number the ordeals it might hold in store? It had taken but a second to make him the most miserable of men—how frightful it was! And why? Why had he blown out the candle? The thought of it depressed him terribly. How could he have brought such disgrace, such everlasting shame, upon his father, who was dearer to him than life itself? Cain had killed Abel, his brother, but he had killed his own father! Ah, what a dreadful thought . . . but had he really wanted to do it? No, he felt as though he had been forced to blow out the candle against his will. The ache inside him had grown too great to be held in any longer . . . for years now he'd felt as though he were a stranger to everything and everyone were a stranger to him . . . and now the fire had flared forth. But why had it done so in a way he hadn't wanted? Why must he profane what was holy to so many people?—It's my curse, he thought, to belong to a nation that has nothing in this world but its religion. This leaves only two choices . . . to attack the faith or defend it . . . and yet all that I want for myself is to be a free man. I can't spend my life being for or against religion . . . there are other things that I want to be, and other things that I want to do for myself and among my people.

He imagined his brief life passing before him. Here were his childhood, his boyhood, and adolescence; here were the ambitions and hopes which lay buried in the fastness of his soul. It had been poor, this life, in the pleasures and amusements of the senses, but it had been rich in fantasies, dreams, visions, and high ambition instead.

One memory stood out among many blurred recollections. It was a summer afternoon; the sun was already low in the sky; he had come home from the heder in an exhilarated mood because the rabbi had favored him especially that day and said that he had

never seen a nine-year-old before with such a marvelous head for the intricacies of the Talmud. The air
had cooled off a bit and felt terribly good and refreshing after the long day shut up in the awful, sweltering
heat of the heder. His path was crossed by a gang of
boys, his friends, and in no time he was standing in
their midst. They ran this way and that, racing together with exuberant cries. Suddenly his father, the
rabbi, appeared on his way to the synagogue for the
afternoon and evening service.

"Nachman, have you prayed yet?"

"I prayed in the heder."

"And why must you run about like that?"

He said nothing.

"Why must you make friends with such foolish
boys?"

He said nothing.

"Come along with me. From now on, we'll pray
in the synagogue together. A Jew mustn't fill his
mouth with laughter in this world. We're here to
worship God and to study His Law; we mustn't even
think of spending our time in such foolery.

"Ah, son, don't you say every day in your prayers, 'And let not the Evil Urge have power over us?'
What a great prayer it is! But the Evil Urge does have
power over us because of our sins. Every moment of
pleasure and enjoyment is put there by the devil to
drag us down into the vanities of this world so as to
rob us of our place in the next. We mustn't take
pleasure, son, we mustn't ever take pleasure in this
world!"

He stared longingly after the gay pack of boys
that continued to romp back and forth. How hard it

was to leave his friends when they were having such good fun! How he had waited and hoped all day long —half choked to death by the heat and the unbreathable air—for just these dear, pleasant moments! But what was he to do? And how could he say "And let not the Evil Urge have power over us" in his prayers tomorrow if he didn't really mean it?

The synagogue. The afternoon service was over. The worshipers had taken candles and placed them upon lecterns to light a Talmud, Mishnah, or other sacred text. A peculiar, hushed sadness reigned in the room. A few men stood near the podium, their books open before them, exchanging an occasional comment or debating some fine point of law. It was terrifically hot. The men's pale, dry lips were caked with dust. The candles burned laboriously, casting a dim light over the interior. And it was here that he would have to spend his favorite evening hours from now on! . . . Only, why did the devil lure him so strongly outside? What could be out there? He recalled the Talmudic text he had learned the other day, which advised: "And if the Evil One accost you on your way, drag him with you to the house of study." . . . —No, he swore, I won't lose my soul like those silly-headed boys who spend all their time in foolish games. I'll fight with the Evil Urge until I drive him from my heart!—But his heart was evil too . . . it kept calling him outdoors until the tears came to his eyes . . . he felt as though he were sacrificing himself to the God of Israel, purifying spirit and soul to worship his Creator. He resolved to dedicate himself body and soul to God and to have nothing more to do with vain, worldly pleasure.—O God, he prayed, make me strong enough to conquer the Evil Urge and to worship You really and truly.—All about him were Jews sitting in study; he alone was without a book. He went to the bookcase to find one and chose a volume that was called *The Beginnings of Wisdom*. His father had told him that every Jew was obliged to know *The Beginnings of Wisdom* by heart and to obey all that was written in it. He leafed through its pages until he came to a chapter that was called "About Hell." The title intrigued him. For years he had heard all kinds of stories about hell and the punishments of the world to come. He wanted to know what the truth really was. He wanted to understand hell exactly, to know what it looked like and what was in it, how big it was and how much it could hold. He wanted to know it all, the whole truth. It was time he found out. He read on.

The congregation was done with the evening prayer; many of the worshipers had already gone home; yet he remained where he was, propped against the lectern. The book lay open before him, but he could have been blindfolded for all that he saw.—So it's all true, he thought. It's true that there's really a hell. And it's true, God, that You really do punish all those who rebel against You. How great You must be, God, how terrible and tremendous, so powerful and so strong that You can do whatever You want—and yet this is how You punish a weak little thing like man!—He felt as though the light had suddenly gone out from his world. How could anyone live in such an accursed, gloomy place? Wherever you went, sin followed after. If you didn't say "amen" the right way after a single prayer, your soul was already damned. If you forgot to wash your hands even once before praying or eating, it was condemned to live in a frog for seven whole years.—It's so terrible, God, it's so hard to live in Your world. Only please, God, don't lead me any more into temptation. Remember that I'm just flesh and blood, and how am I supposed to understand and obey Your whole deep Torah?—He shut his book and rose heavily from his place. A deep groan escaped from him. It was as though a great stone had been laid upon his heart. How oppressive and heavy it felt! And yet this was what the world was like. This was life. He simply hadn't known it until now. . . .

He left the synagogue slowly in a sullen, peevish mood. On the threshold he pulled himself up to his full height, placed a kiss on the mezuzah with the fingers of his right hand, and recited in a whisper, "For he commandeth his angels to guard thee in all thy ways," concentrating as he had been told to on what it said in the holy books about the guardian angel who was born from each commandment one obeyed to help keep one from falling into sin. And yet once outside—the devil himself couldn't have made it more lovely! The great vault of the sky glittered with thousands of bright stars; the pale moon looked down with a kindly, winsome, pitying smile. He was forced to put God aside and to look up at the pure heavens, at the sea-blue valley overhead. The cool, moist air filled him with grudging pleasure and gratification. He thought it so beautiful: the moon, the stars, the blue skies, the shimmer of the rooftops in the moonlight, the trees—it all seemed so simple and right. And yet, ah, how many thousands of ghosts, ghouls, goblins, demons, she-devils, fallen angels, and stray spirits lay in ambush on every side! How much needed to be redeemed in this vile world! And why had he been put in it in the first place? Yes, to redeem as much as he could and to purify his soul —and yet the Evil Urge kept diverting him with foolish amusements and thoughts.

The windows and doors in the street were ajar as he passed. Heads of households sat relaxing by the open windows, eating and drinking after a hard day's work. Women stood in kitchens and cooked dinner over woodburning stoves. Children sat in the doorways or on the ground by the front stoops, eating hot baked potatoes from a communal dish. He walked his solemn way, casting a sorrowful glance at the miserable sinners whom each passing moment brought nearer to perdition. What fools they were to be enjoying a world that was never made for their pleasure! They had forgotten the most important thing of all. His sorrow mounted. Not a person the length of the street was remembering to be mindful of God— how did he know that someday the Evil Urge would not cause him to slip the same way?

He came home feeling fretful and out of sorts. The house was full of light and good cheer. His father, the rabbi, sat at the head of the table, surrounded by a large group of men who were arguing loudly with emphatic gestures. A wit among them was amusing the others with his jokes . . . but ah, what a dreadful sight: his father was laughing! His father was laughing! Hadn't he just told him awhile ago that a Jew mustn't laugh in this world? He looked straight at his face—yes, he really had laughed. He looked again, hoping to find there a flicker of guilt, a prick of remorse for having laughed and forgotten God— but no, he could tell that he'd laughed with a heart that was perfectly clear. He knew that his father, the rabbi, was a good Jew who would yet make up for it with much groaning, fasting, repentance, and confession. Didn't he spend whole nights as it was in tears and penitent prayer and whole days without food? But dear God, why had he forgotten that it was forbidden to laugh? Why had he laughed and at what? What need did *he* have to laugh? And if someone like him could be tricked by the Evil Urge—*his* father, who had worshiped God all his life and never let down his guard against the *klipa* and the "other side"—yes, if even he lacked the strength to vanquish the Evil Urge, what chance was stood by a mere boy like himself?

And at night! Ah, how terrible the nights were! The battles that raged then! How many dreadful warnings were written in the holy books about the nighttime kingdom of the *klipa!* The oil was gone from the lamp. The room was dark. It was terribly quiet. He felt a great weight on his heart. His thoughts were confused and spasmodic. His brain worked at breakneck speed, but he couldn't keep up with it. One thing he knew, however: he was alone by himself in a terrible, black world—he, a weak, lowly boy, was all alone in this dismal world. Thousands of angels and hidden powers lurked all about him . . . the whole world lay in ambush to drag him down to the fiery pit, to hell, and he . . . how weak and lowly he was! He covered his face with the blanket and cried. He felt desperate; it was hopeless; there was no way out. Suddenly a fearful thought crept into his mind and made him recoil. No! It was a sin to even think it. He mustn't. God was good. But why then, the thought went on torturing him, did He create such a terrible world? God was good, but if you didn't wash your hands when you were supposed to, he might turn you into a frog. He made man lowly and weak and expected him to be as strong as Himself.—No, I musn't sin. God is good, good, good. Be gone, you Evil Urge!—He bit his lips, clenched his teeth, pulled his hair in anger at the bitterness of his thought. *Good, good, good,* he deliberately drilled himself; but something inside him spitefully insisted: Either God wasn't good at all, or whoever wrote *The Beginnings of Wisdom* was lying. And how after all did he know? Had he been there himself? But this too, he knew, was the devil at work. It was the Evil Urge provoking him to think blasphemous thoughts about God and the holy *Beginnings of Wisdom . . .*

A sudden ray of light entered from the next room. Through the slightly opened door he saw his father sit down on the floor in a corner. The candle in his hand cast a dim light over the house. His gaunt, suffering face wore a look of sorrow and portentous grief. The corner was alive with an unseen magical field that flowed from it over the house. His father leaned silently on one hand, a terrible sadness in the frozen stare on his guileless countenance. He let out a sigh, and then another and another. A moment passed and he could be heard as he began to chant the midnight vigil in a slow, drear voice.—"Remem-

ber, O Lord, what is come upon us, behold, and see
our reproach."—His voice inched along in a whisper,
word after word. How awful it was!—"O God, the
heathen are come into Thine inheritance; they have
defiled Thy holy temple; . . . they have given the
dead bodies of Thy servants to be food unto the fowls
of heaven. . . . Though Thou hast crushed us into a
place of jackals and covered us with the shadow of
death, if we had forgotten the name of our God, or
spread forth our hands to a strange god. . . . Nay, but
for Thy sake are we killed all the day; we are ac-
counted as sheep for the slaughter. . . . For our soul
is bowed down to the dust; our belly cleaveth to the
earth. . . ."—He eased himself down off his bed and
tiptoed to the door to see his father more closely. It
was a fearful, an awesomely holy scene. The plaintive
chant bore into the recesses of his heart and soul.—
"How long will there be mourning in Zion and weeping in Jerusalem?"—The old man was secretly weeping. Tear after tear rolled down his white beard.—"I
have set watchmen upon thy walls, O Jerusalem,
they shall never hold their peace day nor night."—
He thought of the stories about Jerusalem's walls that
he had heard from Jews who had been there. In his
mind's eye he saw two large teardrops fall from the
Wailing Wall, while a fox ran stealthily in and out of
its breaches. He stood among the ruins by the holy
wall and watched the crowds of Jews as they wept
out loud and threw themselves on the ground. Here
were the remnants of Jerusalem's towers, from a
crumbled mound of which he heard a voice cry out:
"Woe to the father who has sent his children into
exile and woe to the children who are banished from

their father's table!" A veil of darkness covered
Jerusalem. The city lay in mourning. Before a cave
by one of its gates sat the aging King David and
played a frightfully sad and poignant tune upon his
harp. Near him an armed Arab stood guarding the
city, his spear in one hand and his sword on his hip.
High, far away the heavens split open and there was
God himself sitting on His throne and looking down
on the world that served as His footstool. He saw
Jerusalem lying desolate. The throne rocked back
and forth, and two enormous tears hurtled to the
bottom of the great sea. Then all the holy souls who
had martyred themselves in His name came forth
from paradise surrounded by fire, while a river of
blood flowed before them. Their bodies were beaten
and torn; their bony hands were held high and in
them were the scraps of parchment from the Torah
scrolls they had saved from the foe. Before the mercy
seat they flung themselves down, but an awesome
voice called out to them from above: "Return to your
place of rest, ye holy souls, the time has not yet
come!" Then Mother Rachel too fell upon the throne
with a heartrending wail, and the holy fathers pros-
trated themselves at its feet with a terrible cry . . . But
the long, bitter exile was not yet over. Jerusalem was
burned to ashes. The land of Israel lay waste. The
Shekhinah was in exile, and the Jews lay scattered
and dispersed among the nations. Satan reigned vic-
torious. Samael held sway over all. Mikhael, the angel
of Israel, his father had told him, lay bound in chains.
Man was ruled by his passions and couldn't worship
God. Ah, when would the Messiah come? He must
come. No, he must be brought. The Messiah wouldn't

come by himself, his father had said. Each generation must bring him. And yet so many had tried! Joseph de la Reina. The blessed Ari. The Baal Shem Tov. They couldn't bring him because the time hadn't come. But perhaps it now had. It was time to try again. The Messiah must be brought. He must, no matter what!

The candle was nearing its end. The flame burned low, throwing out small bits of wax with a thin sputter. Through the windows of the house the dawn light furtively broke. It grew brighter. The candle had gone out. His father, the rabbi, stood in one corner and read aloud from the Book of Psalms in a drained, gentle voice that seemed to flow through the house. A boundless happiness filled the heart. God's presence, his Shekhinah, was afoot in the house. The whole universe overflowed with His holiness and goodness. The world lay quietly outside the window, sunning itself in God's light. His father had closed his eyes and stood leaning against the doorway as though in a trance, his face radiant with splendor. He seemed to have risen slightly from the ground and to be floating above the floor of the house. He was singing finely and clearly; the soft, thin lilt of his voice was full of a hidden, mysterious power that was easy and light as a childhood dream and terribly sweet to the soul. Now he too was lifted from the ground like his father and hovered in midair. His father soared high toward a fiery stream that ran down the far end of the sky. The fierce light hurt the eyes. His father soared on and on, closer and closer to the terrible stream of fire. The sound of his singing grew stronger and mingled with thousands of other voices of airborne song. The whole world was singing. But the fire grew fiercer and fiercer. The universe was bathed in an ocean of flame. It was hell that was burning so fiercely. Thousands of horrid angels full of eyes, monstrous and ferocious to behold, were transporting hordes of sinful children to be cast into the fire that raged in hell's bowels. Ah, what a dreadful sight! Here was a boy hanging by his tongue. Arms, legs, heads, and torsos tossed on the broiling flames. Now down swooped hideous Satan himself, his red wings blotting out all else. He seized him by a tuft of his hair and began to drag him noisily off to hell. He wanted to cry out, but the flames had burned his lips and he couldn't make a sound. Above him his father was breasting the burning stream . . . he was swimming toward the Messiah . . . no, he had seen him in the devil's grasp and had turned back to rescue him. His father grabbed hold of him firmly. The struggle was savage. His father held on to him by his hand while the devil tore wrathfully at his hair. The terrible pain made him open his eyes. . . . He was lying in bed, surrounded by his father and family.

"Thank God," said his father, the rabbi. "He's opened his eyes."

From that night on—so he remembered—his childhood innocence and animal spirits were taken from him. It was then that he first came to realize that life was a dreadful contest in which he was condemned to struggle and toil for as long as he lived without ever knowing whether he was winning or not. In a vague, undefined way great questions about God, man, and the world now awakened for the first time in his still-unformed mind. They bore there unremittingly, and imperiously demanded an answer. It was then that he first conceived the tremendous idea that it was he who would be the awaited hero, he who would fight the great war and emerge with victory's palm.

A Sabbath eve.

Looking back toward his father's house he saw first the garden, beyond whose fence stretched a broad pond covered with marsh grass. A small stream flowed into the pond at its other end. One of its banks was laced with thick green willows, which stood sadly and dreamily facing the stream, while on the other bank, which was terribly steep and strewn with stark boulders, there grew a small woods embowered in darkness. Frogs croaked in the swamp. Pheasants called. The stream purled in a whisper. Songbirds sang somewhere off in the woods. The leaves and the marsh grass stirred slightly in the wind. Another language was spoken here, different from that of the heder and the rabbi, the synagogue and the marketplace, the house and the street. A fine sun rode haughtily high through the unblemished heavens. The air was pleasant and pure. It was another world here. He felt as though he were looking at a new sky. He had the day off from school, for he had been dismissed from the heder at noon. His father, the rabbi, was making the rounds of the town to gather alms for the poor, after which he would be busy preparing for the Sabbath. Nachman was left free to his own devices. How he loved to spend his idle hours here, in this place! If he daydreamed for a moment in the heder, he would feel the crack of a hand on his cheek and hear the rabbi cry: "Tell me, Nachman, is this the way you do your lessons?" If he walked down the street absorbed in himself, he was sure to bump unexpectedly into some woman who would drop all her things on the ground. If he sat down to eat with his thoughts, a spoon in one hand and a slice of bread stuck in his mouth, a roar of laughter would soon interrupt him. His family thought he was funny. Whereas here—here he could think as much as he pleased unmolested.

It took all his strength to clamber to the top of a steep rock. He stood there looking at the sun, feeling giddy and exhilarated. "Look at me, sun! Look, I'm a hero! I'm going to bring the Messiah!" He brandished his stick in all directions. "Arise O Edom and Ishmael, Arabia and ye Sons of Kedar, Mashma and Duma and Masa, the King Messiah is coming! He's coming, he's coming, I'm going to bring him." A feeling of courage and daring came over him as he stood on the rock and gazed far out into the distance. How high he was above everything! He shook his stick and struck out all around him. He was battling Gog and Magog. The dead lay everywhere. His enemies fell like straws. He fought bravely on, cutting and thrusting. He was a hero like Samson and David. The Philistines whispered his name, for he was the bravest of Israel's warriors. The Sons of Ammon wallowed in their blood, yet he charged again and again, brandishing his stick with every stroke.

He had taken a holy vow before God that he would devote his whole life to bringing the Messiah —but what a difficult task it was. He must conquer Samael and the *klipa*, he must raise up the power of

holiness and crown the King Messiah—and yet he
was only a boy. He remembered the awful moment
when he had sworn the sacred oath and had felt at
once that a terrible burden had come to rest on his
shoulders. But it was already done. There was no
taking it back. Only, how might the Messiah be
brought? He began to search through the holy books,
for everything was in them and no secret could be
kept from them. One need only seek and persevere.
And there was much there that was new to him. The
task was truly great. Even to be a simple Jew one had
to labor mightily; even here the path was hard to
follow and full of thorns. To be a Jew! How demand-
ing it was! For this alone the world had been created
—and yet already Adam had fallen into sin. It had
been too much even for Adam to be a good, simple
Jew who observed the commandments correctly—
and he, a mere boy, wanted to bring the Messiah and
set right Adam's wrong! Adam—so the holy books
said—had brought death into the world, and it was
up to him to bring life. Thousands of generations had
passed, legions of saints had laid down their lives to
bring the Messiah, God's glory seat had trembled in
anticipation—and still the Messiah hadn't come. And
now *he* wanted to bring him. Ah, his vow, his vow!
Whatever happened, there was no turning back. His
vow had long since found its way to heaven. The holy
books said that from every word an angel was born
—a good angel from each holy word and a bad angel
from each bad one. And the bad angels fortified the
klipa and gave it the strength to hold back the Redemption. If he didn't keep his vow, he too would be
abetting the *klipa* against the Redemption instead of

helping to make it come sooner. What a terrible sin that would be! Only, Master of the Universe, what was he to do? How might the Messiah be brought? He had already read many books over and over, yet he still hadn't found a sure clue. The books all spoke about "mystic wisdom," about the cabala, about the Torah being only a "garment," each of whose letters was an entire world in itself. Whoever knew the secret of combining these letters could command all these worlds and bid them to perform his will. The most important thing was to know the uses of the holy names and of the different incantations and their permutations. The whole universe—the heavens, the spheres, everything—rested on the great seventy-two-letter name of God, which was to be found in a hidden verse in the Torah. This name ruled everything, if only one knew how to use it. It was the magic key, and all the world's suffering was only because there was no hero anywhere to seize it and unbar the eternal gate. Foolish men thought that the world was nothing but earth, sky, sun, stars, mountains, rivers, seas, deserts, people, and animals; that pleasure was eating and drinking, talking and laughing, walking and riding; that evil was sickness, hunger, and death; and that courage was physical strength: they saw the world superficially and knew nothing of its hidden inwardness, which the holy books were all about; they thought that the Messiah would come to bring food and drink and the comforts of life to the world. Not at all! The Messiah—so the books said—would come to banish the spirit of uncleanliness, to subjugate Samael and the Evil Urge, and to drive sin from the earth. The books said that if only Jews knew the sorrows of the Shekhinah in its exile, they would not worry about the persecutions of tyrants and the other vain bothers of this world. What mattered, said the books, was spiritual redemption. They said that the Torah must be redeemed from exile. Yes, both the Torah and the holy names of which it was composed were in exile—it was written in the books. When the Messiah came, he would first redeem the letters of the Torah and then the parchment on which they were written; first the soul and then the body; first the Shekhinah and then the people of Israel. Nachman didn't understand all of this too well. Much concerning the Redemption that he read about in the books he didn't understand at all, but it was enough for him to know what the world was really like, what truly mattered, and what was the purpose of all things. He knew now that the soul was everything and the body nothing, and that this world was but a corridor through which the soul must pass to be purified and adorned before entering the chamber where the Shekhinah shone forth in glory. . . .

And yet the task was very great. Weeks and months went by—and still it was beyond him. He didn't even know where to begin. Since he uttered his vow the days had turned into years, into winters and summers, holidays and feast days. How often he had seen his schoolmates happily enjoying themselves without a care in the world. They neither knew nor wanted to know about anything, these boys. Their one accomplishment was to say their prayers every day and prepare their lessons for the heder. They had forgotten all about the Evil Urge, about hell and the Angel of Death, about the Exile, about the Messiah, about the Redemption, about everything. And yet what fun they had Sabbath eves when they bathed in the river and practiced rowing on the water! What splendid times fighting and playing! How merry they were coming home from the heder on winter nights, rolling in the snow and throwing snowballs at each other! They were allowed to do everything, God forgive them, because they hadn't taken a vow. And he? Alas, there were days when he too forgot everything. He all but forgot he was a Jew and foolishly amused himself just like his friends. He too bathed in the river, ran and climbed, took part in horseplay and fights. How it pained him then to remember his vow! He would want to part with his friends at once, but his heart, his heart would keep pulling him back. In another minute he would take his leave . . . yet he couldn't just yet . . . he was having too dear, too pleasant a time. But his vow bore away within him. "How wicked you are!" cried a resounding inner voice. "How can you give up everything for such foolishness? Remember your vow, you wicked boy!" At such times he felt like a battlefield where his good and bad selves were at war. The two of them quarreled and contended with each other, pulling him this way and that, while he stood between them like a golem unable to decide. "Flee while you can, you wicked boy!" urged his good self. "Remember your vow. It's a loathsome, filthy world. Woe to the sinners sunk in vile lusts! Woe to the boys who forget the Master of the Universe and spend all their time in frolic and play! Open your eyes and see how cheap and disgusting such vanities are. Back to

the worship of God, Nachman!" But his bad self
would reply: "Don't be a fool! See what a marvelous
time all the boys are having. Look at that one rowing
so well on the water, and at your friend over there,
the champion in every fight. Everyone is kicking up
his heels and having great fun, and you insist on
being miserable over some nonsense! Who are you to
be worshiping God? Try telling your friends about it
and see how they'll laugh. When you're thirteen
years old and your own master, you'll have to worship God whether you like it or not. Then you'll be
chastised if you don't, but why bother with such silliness now? All the boys are having fun—why not you
too! Do you think you're any wiser or older than
they? Enjoy yourself and let that be enough. You say
there's your vow? But why care about a vow? That
too is just silliness. You can see for yourself that
you're not going to bring the Messiah. How are you
going to bring him? And what makes you even want
to? What are you lacking without him? Why doesn't
somebody else bring him besides you? Who made it
your job? You might at least wait until you're grown
up—then try to bring him if you can!"

. . . He was intently reciting the afternoon prayer
as a Jew should, when one of his friends stole up
behind him and broke his concentration. In the *Shulḥan Arukh* it said: "Let your prayer come first,
though a snake be coiled to strike around your foot."
He struggled manfully not to notice, but the boy kept
teasing him with silly chatter and tried to make him
think forbidden thoughts in the midst of his prayer.
What a great sin that was! The angels refused to accept such a prayer and make it an ornament for the

Holy One Blessed Be He, so that it wandered throughout all the worlds until the demons of destruction snatched it up and made it an ornament for Samael instead. He concentrated on praying as hard as he could, but the boy kept pestering him, poking and pinching and pushing him, and telling him jokes until he burst into laughter in spite of himself and had to rush through the rest of his prayer, swallowing the words just to be done with them. For ever so long now he had sought out a place of retreat every Friday to worship God and search for a way of performing his vow, yet he was still no nearer his goal. . . .

And then, at long last, he found out how to bring the Messiah. In the book *Likkutei Tsvi* he came across a passage that said that "On the Days of Awe, when the cantor is lingering over the melody of the words 'Where is the place of His glory,' one can ask for one of three things: wealth, good children, or the holy spirit." Very well, then: he would not ask for wealth—what did he need it for? What good could it possibly do him? He would not ask for good children either, because he wasn't married yet. But the holy spirit! Yes, he would ask for that. Once it was his, he would be able to bring the Messiah. Nothing was impossible for a man of the holy spirit. The three patriarchs had known exactly when the end of days would come because they were men of the spirit, except that it was taken away from Jacob because he had sought to tell the secret to others. But he would tell it to no one, not even to his little sisters, to whom he was always talking about the Messiah and the Exile. He knew now exactly what to do. Nothing could be simpler. He need only be sure to concentrate all his powers as soon as the cantor started singing "Where. . . ." If he was careful not to be up to some mischief with his friends at that exact moment, the Messiah would surely come. . . .

The Days of Awe arrived. He prepared himself to do everything properly and not falter, God forbid, at the last minute. He knew that one had to be extremely careful, pure and holy oneself for the holy prayer-meditations to work. He called his soul to reckoning and summoned himself to repent. His one fear was that some sin he had committed might stand in his way and keep him from concentrating correctly. He read many pious books of instruction about how to behave during the holy days. With the first sounding of the ram's horn at the beginning of the month of Elul, he could feel God's stern justice descending to earth. The air was filled with trepidation. Hearts trembled in fright at the thought of God's justice. But he felt confident and trustful nonetheless. He could sense how the eternal, never-ending war had reached a crescendo and his soul brimmed within him with longing and powerful faith.

" 'The Lord is my light and my salvation; whom shall I fear? The Lord is the stronghold of my life; of whom shall I be afraid? When evil-doers came upon me . . . even my adversaries and my foes, they stumbled and fell. Though a host should encamp against me, even then will I be confident. . . . Be strong, and let thy heart take courage; yea, wait thou for the Lord.' " He prayed every day with special devotion; he recited chapters of psalms and read in the holy *Shiloh;* he rose at midnight to join the congregation in the penitential service, and when it was over he hid behind the stove in the synagogue and continued to meditate contritely, confessing his sins in a whisper and begging God for forgiveness. In the heder and at home he sat in somber submission like a criminal before the bench. He ate his meals soberly, afraid lest he stumble into sin by eating too grossly, or by wolfing down his food voraciously for the carnal pleasure of it and forgetting that a Jew ate only to sustain himself to worship God, or by omitting to say the grace after meals or to wash his hands before sitting down to the table. Did not every Jew have to remember that his table was an altar, that the food he ate was an offering to God, and that he himself was the priestly sacrificer? Whoever profaned his holy offering deserved to be annihilated in the sight of God.

He bathed every day in the ritual bath. On the eve of the New Year he prayed all day long, recited psalms, read, and behaved in a holy manner. The following morning he rose early. The night had seemed to last forever; he could hardly wait anymore for the great moment to come. He walked meekly to the synagogue, his head bowed submissively low. He neither spoke with nor looked at anyone, lest he sin with his tongue by some lie or offend with idle words. When the cantor came to the Kedushah prayer, his heart began to pound. A storm of emotion broke inside him; his knees buckled with hope and with fear; his scalp crawled and goose pimples covered his skin. It would be any second now. Now the cantor was on the word "Where"—he directed his thoughts as prescribed and prayed for the holy spirit. . . .

He could feel that all had gone well. He had

done everything exactly right. His eyes glowed and the tension subsided. He felt a wave of relief at having faithfully carried out his duty. He finished his prayers with joyful thanksgiving to God, who had granted a mere mortal worm like himself the gift of His spirit. He looked proudly about at the congregation. It was time to start seeking the holy spirit's traces. He began to explore, probing and prodding inside of himself to see if the spirit was growing . . . but no: once was not enough. He would have to concentrate his thoughts on the second day of the holiday too, and on the Day of Atonement as well. He was certain that this was why he couldn't yet feel the spirit's effects. The ten penitential days between the New Year and the Day of Atonement passed with mixed fear and hope. The Day of Atonement passed too, as did the feast of Hoshanna Rabba—and still he searched and probed inside himself to see if there were any signs. But he felt nothing. There was nothing there. He was the same ordinary person as always. The heavens were still their inscrutable selves. Everything was as remote and mysterious as ever. He was no wiser or farseeing than before.

Once again he stood thinking on the craggy ledge by the stream, but his thoughts were no longer the same. He had wearied of bringing the Messiah; his vow was forgotten; his errant passion had perished within him. Sometimes he still remembered the battle he had waged with himself for two full years, and then his mood darkened. He felt ashamed of himself and would have given anything to be able to erase the sad, bitter memories from his mind. The ledge had become his journal: whenever he stood on it, he instantly recalled all he had thought there before. In the freedom of this place, he had let his own mind and soul roam free; alone on his rockbound perch, he imagined himself in spirit to be the omnipotent monarch of all that he saw. At such times his will grew bold and expansive and a mysterious power thrust it ever upward to aerial heights. He felt as though he wanted to fly, to lift and soar from the ground, to challenge and master all things. He—and the sun; he—and the sky; he—and God . . . on the craggy ledge he knew and conversed with them all. What did he care then about the village and its people? What were the boys, the rabbi, and the heder to him? He longed to be a hero, his soul aspired to greatness! An asker of questions would he be and a giver of answers! He wanted to know life's utmost, its ultimate meaning, and to plumb it to the depths. He alternately wept and grew furious with himself in private, and as it were with God too. Dreadful uncertainties stirred in his mind and demanded to be resolved. The Messiah hadn't come. He hadn't been able to bring him. Thousands of Jews had tried, yet none had been able to. A whole people prayed and shed copious tears in order to bring him, suffering cruel exile for his sake; his own father rose every night to pray for his coming—and still he hadn't come. And still the books promised and promised . . .

He was twelve years old already, yet all he could remember having ever heard were stories of suffering and exile, fire and blood, murder and devastation. Martyrs, forced baptisms, slaughtered saints—such was his patrimony. When he was still a small boy his mother had told him that his forefathers had been exiles from Portugal and that his father's father's father was killed in Polonnoye and his father's father in Kamenietz. . . . Now, on the craggy ledge, he thought of the story in the *Midrash Rabba* that he had read with his father on the Ninth of Av about the magnificent children of Jerusalem, those tender, holy babes. Before him stretched the great camp of four hundred boys and girls. They stood on the bank of the broad river, contemplating their captive fate; headlong they hurled themselves into the water . . . Thousands of dramas passed before his eyes. His spirit moved freely through the wondrous places where the little heroes had passed. . . . Who was to say, the frightful thought occurred to him, whether then too, on that very night, the pale moon hadn't looked down serenely as always on the Temple and the city in flames? Had the stars perhaps twinkled in the night sky then too, casting their light on the red pools of blood? Ah, who knew what went on above! Perhaps it was all just a joke. The Bible mocked the customs of the gentiles, but might not the gentiles have a book that mocked the customs of the Jews? Of course, the Jews were not wrong. How could a whole people be wrong? And yet there were seventy nations in the world, of which Israel was only one—was it possible then that all the others were mistaken? There were seventy nations, each with a name and a guardian angel of its own. The world was full of different peoples, each with a god of its own. . . .

He would have liked to tear out his heart together with such thoughts and cast it to the swine.

He wanted to flee, to run away. He was frightened of himself—but where could he flee from himself? He wanted to hide from his dreadful thoughts—but where could he take refuge from the furies of his own mind?

A new scene flashed before him: the synagogue on a summer's day.

Whenever he thought of his boyhood it was of the craggy ledge by the bank of the stream, but when he thought of the adolescent years that came after, it was of the red line of the sunbeam that punctually appeared every morning against the west wall of the synagogue and on the curtain of the holy ark at dusk. Deep within him, where the heroes and saints of his youth were buried, it too lay entombed, this ray of light which had never failed to cheer him when he sat like a hermit over his books and to whisper in his ear: "Just look and see, Nachman, what a big, wide, bright, wonderful world lies just outside the walls of this study house!"

Morning. The sun was not yet abroad. The whole creation lay bound in sleep. A perfect silence prevailed all around. Even the flood of dawn light, which poured into his bedroom and disturbed his sweet slumber with the reminder that it was morning and time to rise and be about his studies, seemed to break with a noiseless ease. His father stood over him to wake him. "Nachman, get up! Let's go to the synagogue to study a chapter together in the *Yoreh De'ah*. Come now, up! Soon your mother will be up too to milk the cow and send her off with the herd. Up now! What are you still drowsing for? The tailors,

the smiths, the tinkers, the builders and the shop-
keepers will soon be up and at their simple work too
—and we by God's grace have the holy Torah for
ours! How lucky we are that the Torah is our only
business—and you still want to sleep? Come now, up
with you! Tell the Evil Urge to be off. Remember the
first sentence of the *Shulḥan Arukh:* 'A Jew must be
as strong as a lion to rise in the morning to worship
his Creator and greet the dawn.'" Yet how sweet
sleep seemed to him then. "Ah, papa," he implored,
"I'll be up in a minute. Just let me be a while longer."
The delicious minutes sped by one by one. With each
he kept rousing himself. He thought of his father
waiting in the synagogue and struggled to rise, reach-
ing out for his clothes that lay on the chair by his
head. Yet some power within him kept pulling him
back and a voice kept repeating: "Why not stay in
bed a bit more? You're so sleepy, and there's still the
whole day in which to study the Torah!" He lay there
with his hands on his clothes, wanting yet unable to
take them until he reminded himself of the first sentence of the *Shulḥan Arukh.* The first sentence—and
even that was too much for him! He dressed himself
quickly lest sleep overcome him once more, washed
his hands with a blessing, and stepped out-of-doors.

It was still quiet outside. The shutters were
closed on the windows the length of the street. The
sky had turned red. The still shadow-laden air was
damp and mild and refreshing to breathe. Cocks
crowed. Cows and goats ambled unhindered in the
streets and doorways of the houses. Before him the
stalls of the marketplace stood fast asleep. A pack of
dogs romped in the open square. Off in the distance

a farmer's cart was approaching. He stood gazing far down each street to where it gave way to gardens and fruit trees. The sight of them filled him with joy. The town was coming to life and beginning to stir. He stood there at peace with himself, contentedly taking all in. The sun peered above the horizon. The sounds and sights in the square kept changing. Suddenly he remembered that his father was waiting in the synagogue—and here he was, squandering his time and neglecting his duty! He hurried onward, seeking to forget all else. Yet the closer he came to the synagogue, the more he felt drawn to the streets, to the gardens, to life. . . . For some time now, ever since he had begun to study daily in the synagogue, he had unwillingly found himself thinking the same unclear thought, which had been on his mind from the day he first crossed the threshold of the building to join those who spent all their days there in pursuit of God's Law. All the while he had felt oppressed by a hidden, elusive emotion. At first it had seemed cloudy and confused, but little by little it had become more and more obvious, more and more transparent. Sometimes he felt as though it were almost within his grasp, and then he grew terribly scared. . . .

He reached the synagogue. The silhouettes of night still lingered inside. The dark lecterns cast a thick pall. The corners of the building were shrouded in gloom, amid which a black figure swayed back and forth. A soft, sad voice made the still air tremble, cutting through the awful silence and filling the building with desolate grief. The figure was his father, who was standing in one corner and reciting psalms. For a moment he completely forgot the grand spectacle that had thrilled him outside. He was standing in a wholly other world. He could feel that he longed to reach out toward something, that a storm of prodigious emotion had been let loose inside him, yet he neither knew what he longed for, nor what he felt, nor what he wanted to reach. Dim visions floated before him. The building seemed to stretch and expand, and in it, as though through a fog, he saw a great universe bursting with the pomp, the pageantry, the drama of the human generations. Thousands of enchantments whispered inside him. He felt both happy and sad without knowing the reason for either. Everything was so befogged. . . .

"Nachman, Nachman!" His father broke into his thoughts.

He took a copy of the *Yoreh De'ah* and went over to his father.

"You're still tired, Nachman. You haven't rubbed the sleep from your eyes yet."

"That isn't so, papa."

"Why do you contradict me? I'm not blaming you for it. You're still a boy, and you haven't yet learned how to fight the Evil Urge. I was once a boy too, and I can still remember struggling with it until I was able to overcome it and to spend day and night in the study of Torah and the worship of God. And yet poor sinners that we are, how many times did the Evil Urge win out over me first! Ah, son, whoever would be a soldier must get used to the smell of sulfur."

"But must everyone be a soldier, papa?"

"Ah, son, son, you've touched the most mortal wound inside me with your question. For years now

I've watched the ways of the world and the path that our people has taken, and this has led me to think no end of sad and despairing thoughts. These thoughts are a great abyss, and I had hoped to leave them to you as my ancestors left theirs to me. But a thought is not something that can be handed down with mere words. Every thought takes hold in the mind only after much contemplation and experience of life. The most that I can do is to try to help you, to give you the key with which you can inherit my thoughts and go on from there, just as I too have gone on.

"You ask me," his father continued after a brief pause, "whether everyone should be a soldier. Ah, son, of course he should, of course everyone should be a soldier! Whoever wants to worship God, whoever wishes to reach the highest goal and carry out the mission for which all life was created, must certainly be a soldier. Whoever wants to pay homage to an earthly king and serve him must be a soldier too. But the kingdom of heaven is like the kingdom of earth. Not every citizen wants to or is cut out to be a soldier. And so the pick of the nation's youth is chosen to serve for all. We too, my son, have been chosen by God to be His soldiers. He has given us His one true Torah, His commandments and His prohibitions, and we have all sworn to be His army, His holy troops. Have you ever thought, son, that while most men are comfortably asleep on soft beds under familiar roofs, an army must camp in tents in the field and suffer from cold, wind, and rain? A soldier must get used to a hard life, to wandering and to lack of sleep, if he is to be able to defend his country and his king. Most of his days are spent in homelessness and in exile; that's what army life is like. One must take good care of one's belongings and guard them from the world, and the more precious something is, the better it must be cared for and the more vigilantly it must be watched. More than three thousand years ago God gave us His Torah and made us His soldiers. We are the army of God and of all that is holy in this world. You're still young, and it's difficult for you to grasp such mysteries. Perhaps when you're older you'll understand. Now it's enough for you to know that we are the soldiers of the Holy One Blessed Be He. God in His grace has given us a very great and precious possession, and He has sworn heaven and earth as His witnesses that we will guard it and defend it for as long as we live. 'For thou art a holy people unto the Lord thy God, and the Lord hath chosen thee to be His own treasure out of all peoples that are upon the face of the earth!' 'Thou hast avouched the Lord this day to be thy God, and that thou wouldest walk in His ways, and keep His statutes, and His commandments, and His ordinances, and hearken unto His voice. And the Lord hath avouched thee this day to be His own treasure, as He hath promised thee, and that thou shouldest keep all His commandments; and to make thee high above all nations that He hath made, in praise, and in name, and in glory; and that thou mayest be a holy people unto the Lord thy God, as He hath spoken.' Yes, Nachman! We are a holy people unto the Lord our God, we are a special people among all the nations on the face of the earth, we are the troops of the Holy One Blessed Be He in this world. *Thou hast avouched the Lord to be thy God,* and *the Lord hath avouched thee to be His own treasure:* ah, son, such are the words of the oath and the covenant that we have sworn to our general! You're still a boy, and you're mostly ignorant of all that our people has been through since it became the army of God. It isn't something you can learn simply by reading the stories and legends in the Midrash, or in the *Yosifon,* or in the *Shevet Yehudah,* or in the *Shalshelet ha-Kabbalah,* or in the *Tsemah David.* Many read these stories, but few are aware of the fruit within the husk, of the depths beneath the surface. Only fools believe that the world revolves by sheer chance, but there are men of simple faith too who can't see beyond the obvious. They know that the Children of Israel were made to suffer in Egypt and labor with mortar and bricks—and so God led them out of there; they know that He tore open His seven heavens in the desert and descended on Mount Sinai to give Moses His Torah; they know that Moses climbed the mountain and remained there for forty days. So what did the children of Israel do? They cast a golden calf and worshiped it as God. Then came the manna, the quail, the wars in the desert, the building of the Temple and its destruction because of idolatry, the Exile and its tribulations. In everything they see only the obvious: that Israel was exiled because it sinned and angered God, and that when our cup overflows the King Messiah will appear to lead us back to our land. Ah, Nachman, my son, it grieves me that I can't reveal more to you. I'm an old, gray-haired man now, and who knows whether God will let me live long enough to tell you more of what I have learned from my masters, and from the holy books, and from His own all-wise hand. The exodus from Egypt, the giving of the Torah—none of it was like what you imagine. I can't tell you how profound it really is. When you grow up you'll read about it in the *Zohar*, and in the works of the Ari and Hayyim Vital, and also in Maimonides' *Guide,* without which you'll never get anywhere. Perhaps then God will grant you the wisdom to understand. The story of the golden calf is not what you think it is—in fact, *The Kuzari* explains how it was really not so farfetched for that day and age, but there's a mystery here too which you can't understand. Idolatry, too, my son, is just a symbol for deeper things. True, if the pagans hadn't prayed to trees and stones, the greatness of Israel for turning its back on idol worship would have been diminished. But the truth of the matter is that human beings were incapable in the beginning of rising to a perception of the sole Creator of the world, and so they began with trees and stones, with unreal forces and false gods, and from the unreal they proceeded to the real, generation by generation, each era drawing closer to the truth. But we children of Israel received the whole truth from God all at once, for we were His special choice and He picked us among the nations to let His spirit dwell among us. Yet because not every Israelite was able to recognize the truth, many turned to other gods, and in this too there are many mysteries. The fact is that in every generation we worship other gods; that is, every generation has its own particular idols. I've already explained to you, son, that we are the soldiers of God—but surely you must have noticed that in every city and in every place the soldiers are outnumbered by civilians who live a completely different life. Were it not for fear of a court-martial, many soldiers who are not committed wholly to their vocation would desert and disappear among these ordinary people. In our army, too, there are in every generation many soldiers who do not understand the mission for which they were intended and are not perfectly devoted to the Lord God of Israel. Such men give themselves over to the worldly pleasures of the civilian life around them. Long after, when the false gods of that time have vanished from the world and are laughed at by everyone, mankind is astonished that its ancestors should ever have worshiped them. But in that age itself nothing could have seemed more natural than to be idolatrous in that way. Ah, son, in order to worship God and keep His holy Torah, one must purify oneself greatly and elevate one's mind so as not to stumble into the worship of idols. You should know that many sparks of holiness descend and fall into the 'other side,' just as sparks from the 'other side' ascend into the camp of the Shekhinah because of our sins. And here too there are great mysteries. There are righteous Gentiles who worship the sparks of holiness that have fallen into the 'other side' and so cleave to the God of Israel, and there are sinful Jews who worship the sparks of the 'other side' that have ascended into the holy and are dragged down to the bottomless pit. But it's too much for you to understand. It's a weakness of mine that I keep mentioning things that I can't possibly explain to you, but remember what I say and think of it when you're older.

"Yes, I'm already an old man, and God only

knows whether I'll live long enough to tell you these things in good time. What I had started to say to you was that I want to bequeath you my thoughts so that you too can become a soldier like me. If only you knew, Nachman, how badly wounded I feel inside. Woe to us who live in fatherless times like these! But why do you look so dismayed? I didn't mean to make you sad. When I contemplate the history of Israel, I see how whenever bad times have come upon us, whenever the Torah has been all but forgotten and our Jewish people has weakened and waned, God has sent us leaders of the flock each single one of whom has been worth the entire nation—men who devoted their talents, their time, their wealth, and their strength to the welfare of Israel and the glory of the Holy One Blessed Be He. Whenever I read the books of Prince Don Isaac Abrabanel and Rabbi Menasseh ben Israel—ah, son, here were real soldiers for you! Soldiers! It's easy enough to be a soldier in the barracks in peacetime, but how hard it is to be a soldier in wartime when all around you the army is retreating and giving ground. They gave up everything— their lives, their fortunes, their honor—to martyr themselves for God. You, Nachman, are in the line of eight generations of rabbis and a direct descendant of Menasseh ben Israel. Our holy ancestors were true soldiers who shed their blood like water that God's will be done, and it's my wish that you should one day be a rabbi too. Son, I too was once a peacetime soldier. I remember how as a boy I was far from being the only one to reach the study house before dawn. Now this building stands deserted, but then it was filled with prayer and learning from end to end. Nobody comes here anymore in quest of God. Nowadays the young boys are all in the government schools, where they worship the idols of our times . . . woe to us who have lived to see it happen! Our army is crumbling. There's no one to stand in the breach and turn back the tide. Woe, woe is us! I'm afraid, son, that you too may falter like them. One must rise above everything, forget everything, give up everything! One must know that everything besides one's mission is a frivolous waste! One must know that the Torah alone is important and that all else beside it is vanity and foolishness! One must be a soldier. . . . Come now, it's time we studied."

It was then that he was robbed once and for all of his remaining childhood peace.

A soldier! A soldier! The word rang like a bell in his ear. He was just now beginning to grasp what his father wanted from him.

He wanted him to become a soldier, to war with Satan and the Evil Urge, to devote his whole life to his people and his faith; he wanted him to give up all and to forget all; he wanted him to know that the Torah was everything and that everything else was nothing . . . nothing . . . he himself was nothing . . . how terrible it was to serve in such an army!

The synagogue—his father had said so himself—was deserted. All the boys had gone off to school. And he? Here he still sat with his books and his aging father. . . .

The same vague thought that had troubled him ever since he had begun his studies in the synagogue was now growing clearer in his mind. He had yet to confront it in all its awful immensity, but he was beginning to understand why it bothered him most when he sat by himself in the still, dreary building and watched the sun's rays pierce its walls with their dazzling hues, or when he dallied by himself on the craggy ledge while the image of the synagogue rose before him. Yes, he thought he now understood why each day of the week that he sat watching the sunbeams in the synagogue he thought of the boys, his old friends, who had gone off to school, while each Sabbath eve that he slipped off to his rock to delight in the splendor of nature, he thought of the synagogue, the old study house, and of his father inside it . . .

Afternoon. It was frightfully hot outside. The streets were practically empty. His body craved rest. He felt terribly sleepy and kept wanting to nod and doze off. A dead silence pervaded the synagogue. The lecterns scattered about the building looked like tombstones over graves. The books rested listlessly in place on their shelves. In a corner against the east wall the village idler, Alter, sat in a mindless trance, automatically scratching one end of his pointy beard. His eyes floundered in the open book that lay before him, amid letters that would not become words. He sat without a sound as always, sunk in thought, or rather in its frozen, apathetic absence.

Nachman went to the bookcase, picked out a volume of the tractate Bava Kama, and went over to one of the lecterns. The sages of old advised the young student to sharpen his wits on torts, and so his rabbi had counseled him to study the code of Nezikin, of damages and claims. He stood leaning against

the lectern, his head propped on his hands above the
text. A kaleidoscope of colors, lights, and dim imagin-
ings whirled before his eyes. The letters rose from
the page of the Talmud to dance before him as thousands of reddish dots. There was a ticking in his brain;
his eyelids sought to close; a light, pleasant weight
bore down on his chest. To be able to sleep now! To
hear the delicate music of a songbird hidden away in
its nest, to lie by a running stream on a bed of soft
grass in the shade of green trees, to stare peacefully
at the deep blue sky without thought or desire for
hours on end, to listen with perfectly innocent, tran-
quil, childlike joy to the wonderful symphony of
noises that filled God's world! His soul was still weary
from his morning lesson with his father. The latter's
words grated strangely and harshly in his ears, and a
swarm of confused memories swept through his
mind. He was ridden by fragments of feeling that
came from and led to nowhere. How dull the Talmud
now seemed! How very dull! The veil of desolate
mourning that hung over the building was too awful
for words. The dead! They were everywhere. Yet
how fully alive were the skimming sunbeams outside!
He must get away. Barely a footstep from here everything was brimming with life. He glanced inadvert-
ently at Alter in the corner and a frightful thought
crossed his mind. This too, he mused, was a soldier.
Yes, here was the model soldier his father wanted
him to be, this gaunt, haggard idler who spent all his
days slumped in a dark corner of the study house,
staring at a book before him with bloodshot, ignorant
eyes! What a marvelous army it must be that enlisted
soldiers like Alter! A bitter smile played over his lips.

The depressing thought brought tears to his eyes. He recalled the story he had recently read in the Book of Judges about Jephthah and his daughter, and how he had wanted to cry then too. How strange it all was! He was no longer a boy, after all; he could follow the most complicated legal reasoning; his father had told him that he might soon complete the first course of talmudic studies; his fellow townsman had begun to visibly honor him, many had even taken to boasting of him aloud; and yet still he continued to be fond of the childish tales in the Bible such as those in Samuel and Judges. Here were books in which there wasn't a single difficult passage—yet how he loved them all the same. They had a different flavor that was not of the synagogue—a flavor of freedom, of late Friday afternoons before the Sabbath, of the woods behind the town on Lag B'Omer. . . . His thoughts returned to Jephthah and his daughter. Jephthah too had been a soldier. "And Jephthah vowed a vow unto the Lord, and said: 'If Thou wilt indeed deliver the children of Ammon into my hand, then it shall be, that whatsoever cometh forth of the doors of my house to meet me, when I return in peace from the children of Ammon, it shall be the Lord's, and I will offer it up for a burnt-offering' . . . and, behold, his daughter came out to meet him with timbrels and with dances; and she was his only child; beside her he had neither son nor daughter . . ." How dreadful it was! Yet she was a soldier's daughter. "And she said unto him: 'My father, thou hast opened thy mouth unto the Lord; do unto me according to that which hath proceeded out of thy mouth; forasmuch as the Lord hath taken vengeance for thee of thine enemies, even of the children of Ammon.' " . . . But how wonderful, how beautiful, had been her last request! "Let me alone two months, that I may depart and go down upon the mountains, and bewail my virginity, I and my companions." . . . A wave of longing swept over him. He was jealous of Jephthah's daughter. Behold the mountains and valleys matted with grass, the summer days, the pure, good air, the cooling shadows of the hills, the cold, cold springs in the hollows to gladden the soul! She went for long walks with her friends, lost in sweet pleasure, while her father waited to perform his vow. . . . He suddenly remembered what his own father had told him about having to be a soldier. He too was being asked to forget and give up all, yet to him it was not even granted to wander among the mountains and weep for his youth. He must remain shut up with the more-dead-than-alive Alter, who swayed back and forth day and night like a black apparition over the Talmud that was forever open before him.—No! he thought. I wasn't meant to be a grave-tender. I won't be such a queer kind of soldier. I want to live like everyone else and not be buried alive here with Alter the Idler! —He glanced down at the Talmud before him, which was wet with his tears. It suddenly struck him that he had neglected his lesson and let an entire hour go by in unworthy thoughts. He drove them from his mind and plunged into his text once again.

Three hours went by in uninterrupted study. The passage before him was unusually difficult and complex. The various commentators fought over the Law with vigor and determination, one an immova-

ble mountain of erudition, another a force irresistible
in its brilliance. How fondly he enjoyed the clashes
among them! His melancholy vanished; his spirits
soared; gladly he gave himself over to the depths of
the Law. By dint of his own efforts he was able to
anticipate the query of the *P'nei Yehoshua* and to
harmonize it with the rebuttal of the Maharsha. He
was bursting with exhilaration. Triumph followed triumph; proud bastion after bastion toppled to the
ground. He scaled height after height, building and
destroying whole worlds with a puff of his breath.
Nothing could stand in his way. The printed letters
on the page sparkled like jewels. He felt gratified and
content. He heart lay reconciled within him, lacking
nothing. There was nothing more for it to want. Here
was happiness at last.

He reached the end of the passage and sat down
to rest, yet his mind would not remain still. How
magnificently deep the *P'nei Yehoshua* was—and yet
he had been able to foresee its very words! Who was
to say that he too would not one day be another *P'nei
Yehoshua,* a master commentator? Only, how could
he have let himself lose so much time in unworthy
thoughts? How could he have felt jealous of the boys
in the government schools and thought so little of the
study house and of the holy Torah—God's beloved
Torah, which was as deep and full of pearls as the sea!
The *P'nei Yehoshua,* the Maharsha, the Maharram
Shif, even the simplest qualification of Rashi or the
rejoinder of one of his disciples! And he had actually
wanted to leave all this, the wonderful and incompa-
rable pleasure of the Law! How meek he now felt. He
thought of the fetching homilies in the Midrash.

"Come, my beloved, let us go forth into the field; let us lodge in the villages. Let us get up early to the vineyards; let us see whether the vine hath budded, whether the vine-blossom be opened, and the pomegranates be in flower; there will I give thee my love. . . ." " 'Come, my beloved, let us go forth into the field.' Thus said the Daughter of Israel to the Holy One Blessed Be He: 'Master of the Universe, judge me not as Thou judgest the dwellers of cities who are rife with theft, licentiousness, and vain perjured oaths.' " " 'Let us go forth into the field'—'Come and I will show Thee Thy scholars, who toil without respite over Thy Law.' 'Let us get up early to the vineyards'—These are the synagogues and the study houses. 'Let us see whether the vine hath budded'— These are the Masters of the Law. 'Whether the vine-blossom be opened'—These are the Masters of the Commentaries. 'And the pomegranates be in flower' —These are the Masters of the Homilies. 'There will I give thee my love'—'There will I show myself to You in my glory, honored among my sons and daughters.' " How fond he was of the dialogues between the Daughter of Israel and the Holy One Blessed Be He! The Daughter of Israel was a fair and tragic maiden dressed in mourning, who threw herself weepingly, imploringly, longingly, with childlike innocence, before her kind old father, the Holy One Blessed Be He, whose cruelty toward her was only a seeming show, for even when He rebuked her His voice was full of mercy and forgiveness. . . . Whenever he came on such legends, an indescribably bittersweet lump would form in his throat. As though through a fog he saw the downtrodden, destitute

Daughter of Israel. Around her was strung the bead-
work of awesome, magical tales which he had read or
heard told. His soul burst with passionate yearning
for the sorrowful sight. He felt disgust for his own
dull life and a voice as though called out within him
for tears, more tears. No pain, no ordeal, could be too
much. Strike, burn, stoke high the fires! Let him too
see the pyres and the rivers of blood! Let him share
the bliss of the slaughtered saints! Let him bravely be
the one to cut the throats of his brothers and sisters
and cry "Hear, O Israel, the Lord our God, the Lord
is one" with a smile of contempt! Let him too martyr
himself on the sword!

To think that the boys in the government schools
could forget all this!

He thought of what his father had told him about
wanting to leave him the thoughts he had inherited
from his forefathers so that he too could hand them
on down. What thoughts had he meant? No doubt
they were of this very chain of trials, tortures, and
persecutions that ran down the generations, this al-
bum of the never-ending war that a father must give
to his son, from the first casting out of the Exile to the
present day. Yes, this was what his father had meant
when he had asked him to be a soldier. He wanted
to entrust him with his thoughts, and so he had asked
him to be a soldier that he might be able to defend
them, for without a struggle they could not be protected and passed on. He now began to understand
his father's warning that he not be taken in by the
idolatry of the times. Why, just a few hours ago he
had done just that, he had envied the boys who had
gone off to school and belittled God's Torah! It was

certain that these boys would never inherit or hand on their fathers' thought; *they* would never be taught to be Jewish soldiers. . . .

Yes, his father had been right to rail against the times and to have said this morning that once he had been a peacetime soldier but that now everything had changed. If he envied anyone now, it was the brave soldiers who had forgotten and given up all for the will of God and the welfare of Israel. As though in a vision the bright portraits of these mighty men of arms passed before him. Here was Rabbi Akiva, whose skin the Romans had flayed with steel combs. Here was Rabbi Yosi, whose flesh they had pierced like a sieve because he had taught the forbidden Law to his five disciples. Here were the last defenders of Beitar. Here were Rabbi Yehudah Halevi, Abrabanel, Menasseh ben Israel, the Ari, the Baal Shem Tov, the Baal Or Hayyim, the Rabbi of Berditchev, the Maggid of Mezritsh, and all the other heroes through the ages who had truly forgotten and given up all. Not for them the indolent hearth; with the wanderer's staff in their hand and God's Law in their breast they had uprooted themselves from nation to nation and from kingdom to kingdom in order to observe the Torah and defend it. Then there had been heroes everywhere, whereas now he stood alone. Yet he would not leave his post. He swore to the Lord God of Israel to serve Him as long as he lived. . . .

Two more years passed. He was sixteen years old, and still he sat all day long with his father and Alter in the synagogue. Yet how much to think about there had been in these years, and how greatly his mind had grown!

He remembered how this intellectual change had begun. He had come on a copy of Rabbi Boruch Kossover's *The Foundations of Faith* and had been engrossed by this book, which explained the principles of the cabala in an easily understood manner that was spiced with quotations from Maimonides' *Guide to the Perplexed* and from the works of Levi ben Gerson. He had repeatedly racked his brains over the mysteries of *tsimtsum* and *hitpashtut*, God's mystic contraction and expansion, and over His being called *En-Sof*, The Infinite One, and The Purposeless One, *Bilti-Baal-Tachlit*. Little by little he had supplemented his knowledge of the cabala with the *Guide* itself, Yehudah Halevi's *Kuzari*, and Levi ben Gerson's *The Wars of the Lord*. The profound idea that "the will of God is universal and immutable, for were it subject to change this would detract from His total perfection" gave him no peace. Only the walls of the synagogue, between which he paced back and forth all day long, and his bed at night on which he tossed and turned, were witness to his conflict. The struggle was grim and relentless. Within his frail heart all that was holy and precious was at war with all that was holy and precious. He realized then that not only did Evil do battle with Good, but that Good itself had many different shades and parties which fought among themselves. Previously he had known that Maimonides, Nachmanides, Abraham Ibn Ezra, Rashi, Rabbi Levi ben Gerson, David Kimchi, Abrabanel, the Narboni, Samuel ben Adret, Rabbi Samuel ben Meir, Abraham

ben David, Yedaiah ha-Penini, Joseph Caro, and
Rabbi Azariah of the Adumim were all holy men
whose commentaries were as tried and true as the
Law itself. Yet now that he had begun to delve into
their works, he discovered that their views were as
far apart as east was from west, and he was left to
wander like a lost soul among them.

He might be reading Maimonides' *Guide.* Profiat Duran, the Narboni, and Hasdai Crescas had all
sought in their commentaries to elucidate its hidden
sense. The passage in question was terribly deep, its
contents most grand and sublime—and here was
Abrabanel declaring that these other commentators
were complete heretics who didn't understand
Maimonides one bit! Or take the feud between Rabbi
Judah Alfachar and David Kimchi, or that between
Samuel ben Adret and Yedaiah ha-Penini. How ab-
sorbing, how poignantly moving was Yedaiah's letter
to ben Adret! He defended his opinions like his own
life; he pleaded and raged, wept and spoke daggers,
and each single word was torn from his heart. But
Samuel ben Adret was a great man too and he fought
back with all the power at his command. Or the duel
between Joseph Caro and Azariah of the Adumim!
They neither asked nor gave any quarter, and Rabbi
Joseph did not shy from using the most terrible
weapon of all: the sword of excommunication. And
why? Because Azariah had dared question the
veracity of a story in the Midrash. Alas, how culpably
Nachman himself had thought about such stories in
recent days! Indeed, all of these warring scholars
chose their weapons from the Midrash, which each
interpreted as he pleased, so that one man's or-

thodoxy was sinful heresy in the eyes of the next. What a tremendous difference of opinion there was between Rabbi Abraham, Maimonides' son, and Joseph Caro! Nachman himself was partial to Rabbi Abraham, just as he was to Levi ben Gerson, whose definition of prophecy as "the workings of the active intellect" seemed so natural and clear . . . except that the scholars who opposed it insisted that such "prophecy" was a flat denial of divine revelation, and even Maimonides had ruled that whoever denied the divine origin of the Law had no share in the world to come. How sorry this made Nachman feel for himself! Because of a single thought he stood to lose all, even his share in the world to come. He strove to suppress his awful suspicions once and for all, but as though to deliberately spite him a new one entered his mind.—You fool! it mocked. What can you lose? What makes you think that there's a world to come at all? If the Torah doesn't come from God, then neither does anything else, so what is there to be lost? —He was partial to the theory of the active intellect; he was most drawn of all to the philosopher Levi ben Gerson; but why? Was it not just because here was a broad back to hide behind, an authority on whom to pin his own heretical doubts concerning God's Law and His relations with man? Yes, he was a heretic! He himself had not known until now what had been happening inside him, what his own thoughts had been and where they had been leading. For two years now he had been lost on this dark, dismal path without even knowing. . . .

Even before this a ghastly question had begun to torment him and disturb his devotions.—Nachman, a voice deep within him had called whenever he had risen to pray, whom are you trying to fool? To whom are you praying and why? Do you really mean to say that you can still believe in a God who listens to everyone's prayers?

He had continued to observe the commandments minutely, down to the most trivial one; he had even been able to justify them to himself; but prayer, to pray—ah, why had he still gone on praying? To whom?

And then one night—a shudder still passed through him when he remembered that dark night of reckoning—he put all the thoughts of these last two years together, adding up each doubt or conclusion that he had read of or arrived at himself, so that before dawn broke a light had been cast into the darkest crannies of his soul, and he suddenly knew that without having wanted it, without having known it, he had become someone else whose thoughts and feelings could not be controlled anymore. It was no longer in his power to bend them to his will.

When he arose the next morning, he knew that he no longer had a God. He didn't pray that whole day, not even the "Hear, O Israel" or the grace after meals.

It was the eve of the fast of the Ninth of Av, the day of mourning for the destruction of the Temple. Despair and sorrow were written on his father's face. The old man walked back and forth in the house with a preoccupied air, his shoulders stooped and his eyes on the ground. The books that were allowed to be read on the fast day had already been set out on the

table: Job and Jeremiah, the midrash on the Book of
Lamentations, the tractate Mo'ed Katan, and others.
A spirit of special sadness had settled over the silent
house. The women prepared the pre-fast meal and
argued with each other over what foods were per-
missible for the occasion. People passed somberly in
and out of the house as though visiting a mourner,
without pausing to say hello or good-bye. The street
outside the window had a different look too. Children roamed about in it with play wooden swords.
The women hurried from house to house, busy with
the meal and with getting out their hour books in
which they would follow the chanting of the Scroll of
Lamentations in the synagogue and read about the
destruction of God's house. The children would have
liked to be carefree and flourish their wooden swords
on this day that they had off from school, but they
knew it was forbidden. "What makes you so merry
today?" their mothers had demanded. "Is it because
our Temple was destroyed? This is no day for fun and
games!" A group of boys had formed a circle on the
street corner and were retelling the story of the evil
lizards who had helped to burn down the Temple
. . . Yet Nachman felt remote from it all. He was no
longer the person he should be or that others still
thought that he was. He had become someone else.
All was lost. Everyone seemed a stranger. If only his
father knew that for the first time today phylacteries
had not touched his son's head! If only he knew that
this son was a heretic, an unbeliever! If he knew that
he would be mourning tonight not for the destruction of the house of God, but for the ruin of his own
house, his life and dreams. . . . Why couldn't he look

his father in the face? Why couldn't he look at any-one? He wanted to confess everything, he must! Why did everyone still pay him such deference? Why did they treat him so kindly? Their every word pierced him like a knife. He was a liar, a hypocrite, a swindler. If only there was one living soul to whom he could bare his inner life, who would know and understand what he was going through. How happy it would make him to be able to believe that God above was looking down on his sorrow and comprehending his pain.

It was dusk when he reached the synagogue. The building was packed with men as though on a holiday, yet all wore their workaday clothes. The benches had been turned upside down. The lecterns lay on the ground. The holy ark stood bare, stripped of its embroidered drape. A tallow candle burning on the cantor's podium cast its dim light over the crowd of men seated barefoot on the floor. The cantor chanted the evening prayer to the melody of the Book of Lamentations, which bleakly filled the half-lit building with a melancholy woe. Everyone but himself was absorbed in the evening prayer. From now on, he had made up his mind the night before, he would pray no more. The entire worshipful congregation was one heart and he another. He was cut off from the House of Israel, banished from among his own people. How terribly he would have liked to rejoin them! He would have given his life to do it. But how was it possible? He had sundered the bonds of his own free will and could never mend them again.

The prayer was over. The large congregation remained on the ground, each man with a candle in his hand and the Book of Lamentations before him.

The cantor sat on a stone before the podium and read from the scroll in a low, drear voice. Nachman glanced about the building. All were intently following the words of the chant in their books. Now and again a faint sigh could be heard. His father sat near him, staring in his book with unseeing eyes. Tear after tear dropped from his cheeks to the old lamentary, which was stained with tears and tallow already. The cantor sang on. A great sea of trials, a sea of tears, burst from the throat of this simple man. Every word was a wave of suffering and pain, a stormy breaker that crashed upon the shore. Wave called to wave and trough to trough. "O wall of the daughter of Zion, let tears run down like a river day and night; give thyself no respite; let not the apple of thine eye cease. Arise, cry out in the night, at the beginning of the watches; pour out thy heart like water before the face of the Lord; lift up thy hands toward Him for the life of thy young children, that faint for hunger at the head of every street. . . ."

The cantor read on. "I am the man that hath seen affliction by the rod of His wrath. . . . My flesh and my skin hath He worn out; He hath broken my bones. . . . He hath made me to dwell in dark places, as those that have long been dead. He hath hedged me about, that I cannot go forth; He hath made my chain heavy. . . . He is unto me as a bear lying in wait, as a lion in secret places. . . ." And yet this man was actually happy! "This I recall to my mind, therefore have I hope. Surely the Lord's mercies are not consumed, surely His compassions fail not. . . . The Lord is good unto them that wait for Him, to the soul that seeketh Him. It is good that a man should quietly wait for the salvation of the Lord. It is good for a man that he bear the yoke in his youth. Let him sit alone and keep silence, because He hath laid it upon him. Let him put his mouth in the dust, if so be there may be hope. Let him give his cheek to Him that smiteth him, let him be filled full with reproach. For the Lord will not cast off for ever. For though He cause grief, yet will He have compassion according to the multitude of His mercies. For He doth not afflict willingly, nor grieve the children of men. To crush under foot all the prisoners of the earth, to turn aside the right of a man before the face of the Most High, to subvert a man in his cause, the Lord approveth not. Who is he that saith, and it cometh to pass, when the Lord commandeth it not? Out of the mouth of the Most High proceedeth not evil and good? Wherefore doth a living man complain, a strong man because of his sins? Let us search and try our ways, and return to the Lord. Let us lift up our heart with our hands unto God in the heavens. . . ." No, such a man had never seen real affliction in his life. So good, so trusting, so hopeful a heart, which, in the very act of turning its cheek to Him who smote it, was certain that though He caused grief yet would He have compassion according to the multitude of His mercies; so innocent a heart, which was willing to be comforted before it had even done mourning; so whole a heart was healthy and strong, stronger than Jerusalem's walls. The walls of the city had been razed by the foe, but this heart? This heart had remained unscathed. When the floodgates had opened all around it, it had not stopped to philosophize whether the will of God was immutable or not.

Then his soul grew bitter within him.—Ah, he

demanded, why have they robbed me of the Lord
who is good unto them that wait, to the soul that
seeketh Him? Why have they robbed me of the
brave, the mighty and terrible Lord who breaketh
the cedars of Lebanon and maketh them dance like
sheep, the merciful Lord who restoreth the humbled
in spirit, who knoweth what lieth in darkness while
his people dwelleth in light? Give me back my God,
the God of the Jews! The God of Aristotle can do
nothing for me. He is a figurehead, a king without a
kingdom, not a God who lives. Give me a God who
rules, who "loveth the stranger, in giving him food
and raiment." Give me back the God who is near to
me and I to Him! The God of Abraham, Isaac, and
Jacob, the God of Moses and the prophets, the God
of all this holy congregation that is melting in its tears
for the destruction of Jerusalem while its heart trusts
and hopes that God will rebuild Zion and gather the
scattered remnants of Israel from the far corners of
the earth. . . . Take what you want from me—heaven
and hell, my share in the world to come—but give
me back my light, my heart, my soul, my people, my
God! Why should anyone care if there is a God in
heaven or not? It's enough to know Him in one's own
heart, to feel Him there every second. Ah, the heart,
the heart! Judge for yourselves, you philosophers:
here is the heart that you have labored to produce—
and here is the heart that is the labor of Moses and
the Prophets. . . .

The cantor was done with the chant. One by one
the congregation drifted home. His father sat on the
floor in a corner by the east wall surrounded by the
village elders, to whom he read aloud from a passage

in the *Midrash Rabba.* A terrible stillness engulfed
the building, which was steeped in murk. His father's
low voice mingling with the sighs that burst from the
elders blanketed all with a horrible woe. Nachman
sat on the ground, forgetful of all he had been thinking, his head in his hands, his eyes upon his father, his
mind a perfect void. . . . Suddenly he stirred and cast
an uncertain glance over the synagogue. The sight
seemed strange and new to him; his scattered
thoughts began to regroup. One by one his memories
of the past twenty-four hours flew home to roost,
joining to form a large and dismal likeness. How he
wanted to forget them, to erase them from his mind
with one stroke, to be reborn a wholly different,
wholly other person!

He glanced again at his father. Without knowing
why, he thought of a story he had once heard told as
a child. Many hundreds of years ago there had lived
a certain brave and beloved king. This king was a
great ruler, and he conquered many lands, islands,
and oceans until he held sole sway from Africa to Ind.
He also had an only son, a fine, bright lad, who was
a brave warrior himself. When the young prince
grew up, he fared forth to continue the wars of his
father and subdued even more great and powerful
nations. One day, when he was traveling through far
India, he spied the daughter of the Indian king and
desired her for his wife. But the king of India refused
to give him her hand. Then the prince summoned his
army and went to war. The war lasted many months
and years; thousands of men were killed, tens of
thousands wounded; widows, orphans, and bereaved
parents grew as common as the sand by the sea. Fi-

nally, the last fortress surrendered. The prince and his army broke into the king's palace—and behold, there was the princess lying dead on the floor. . . . The soldiers went home. The old king had died long ago. Generations came and went, and still the prince stood in the desolate palace and wept for his lost love. The entire city and the countryside around it had lapsed into crumbling ruins. A wrathful God's curse had come to rest wherever the prince had trod, yet still he lived on, bitterly weeping day and night before the body of his beloved. . . .

Ah, how frightful it was, and yet it was so! He looked at his father and at the elders gathered around him, weeping for their beloved like the tragic prince. Generations had come and gone; entire nations had died and been born; continents and oceans had been transformed; millions of human beings had lived and died, fought and made peace, hated and loved; the wheels of life had spun round with their mighty sound; and there stood the prince in his desolate corner, forsaken and alone. What did time, the human generations, the nations of the world, mean to him? He stood and wept for his beloved. . . .

Ah, the tragic prince! As far back as he could remember his father too had lived in distant lands, among the ruins of Zion and Jerusalem, among the forgotten spirits of the dead, the ghosts of his teachers and forefathers. His every word, thought, dream, hope, and aspiration had been of these forsaken ruins and forgotten ghosts. Among them he had passed his whole life. Among them he had brought up his son.

He now understood the dim thought that had first crossed his mind when he began to study in the

synagogue. Already then he had felt that he was living in a world not his own. This feeling had pursued
him all the time and filled him with foreboding about
his future. Now it was obvious, as clear as day. . . .

"Nachman!" his father called out, approaching
him unawares.

"What?" he exclaimed. He felt as though he had
just awakened from a deep sleep.

"Nachman, Nachman," his father admonished,
the flicker of a smile on his lips, "is it Jerusalem you're
mourning for? 'Thus saith the Lord of hosts: My cities
shall again overflow with prosperity; and the Lord
shall yet comfort Zion, and shall yet choose Jerusalem.' Son, son, the land of Israel is nothing but earth
and dust. Jerusalem is just a city of houses, markets,
and towers. The Temple itself was only a large building, with great slabs of marble and much silver and
gold. What more was there? Here too, praise God, we
have large buildings and synagogues. Once our synagogue burnt down with all its Torah scrolls—you
were just a small boy at the time—and I didn't even
weep or mourn. But once I overheard an ignorant
Jew swear vulgarly at a scholar, and I tore my clothes
and fasted all day. . . . Do you understand, son, do you
understand?"

"But for what are you mourning tonight, then,
papa?"

"For what? I'm mourning because at the same
time that Titus ravaged the Jerusalem of earth, the
spirit of Rome, as it were, ravaged the Jerusalem of
heaven. Yes, when we were driven into exile, so was
. . . but you know what else was exiled with us. I don't
want to have to put it in plain words . . . everything

is in exile . . . holiness itself is in exile . . . all the spiritual powers of our people are in exile, bound in the clutches of Samael and his crew. The Holy One Blessed Be He never requites Himself on a nation unless He requites Himself on its guiding spirit first, and though our own guide is the Shekhinah, since we have no other god beside Him, He still chose to deal with us in this manner, which we musn't question. And so our hands are tied and there is nothing we can do for ourselves, because our powers are enslaved to Samael and aren't ours to command. Our very existence depends entirely on prayer and the commandments, through which we must try to recapture the divine flow of grace from the days when the Temple still stood and the Shekhinah was not in captivity. To what can I compare it for you? It's like a rich man who has lost his whole fortune yet hopes to make it all back. What does he do with himself now that he has been ruined? Every minute of the day he seeks to keep alive the memory of the comforts and refinements that were his when he still had his wealth. So we too are ruined in the Exile, because Samael has stopped all the channels that lead to holiness, so that we would have died a spiritual death, God forbid, or nourished ourselves from the *klipa* (for the spirit must nourish itself just like the body), if it weren't that by recalling the divine flow from the days when our Temple still stood, we can manage to survive the Exile until the Redemption has been wakened. Yet until then we are helpless, because our spiritual powers are in exile and in thrall to Samael, which is what the rabbis meant when they said that 'The prisoner cannot free himself from his own cell' " . . .

"Ah, papa, papa!"

"What, Nachman? Is there something you wanted to say?"

"Ah, papa, I'm afraid that I won't be able to explain myself to you, or the way I understand what you've been saying and hinting. Papa, I've always tried to remember your words and to think of them all the time, and the more I think of them, the more I find in them. And yet somehow I feel that I'm not explaining them to myself in the same way that you meant them. You said just a minute ago that holiness is in exile and that our spiritual powers have been captured by Samael. You told me a parable about a rich man, and you said that we have no resources of our own in the Exile and must be content to remember God's grace from the time when the Temple still stood. Say what you will, it sometimes seems to me that I can see our whole Jewish people sitting and weeping over graves for the last two thousand years without having anything to do with life itself. You said there's nothing we can do for ourselves. Of course there isn't! Whoever spends all his time in the graveyard, away from life, certainly can do nothing for himself. You yourself can calmly wait for the Redemption. But it's too much for me any longer! I can't go on chanting forever, 'Every town stands proud on its foundation, but the City of God lies low in desolation' " . . .

"That's enough, Nachman!" his father said harshly. "Don't be insolent to God! How can you use such language? Go to sleep, or take a book and read."

His father went silently to a corner of the synagogue and sat down. Nachman continued to think.

In his mind's eye he saw the wretched masses who were now sitting on the ground in thousands of synagogues all over the earth—a great, wandering, ill-starred people, standing forever by some ruin, weeping, weeping . . . how long it had been standing there! Lord God, how much longer must it go on? He was certain now of the answer to his interminable questions about the synagogue, about the Talmud and its commentaries and all the logical exercises upon them. As much as he had loved these holy books, as greatly as he had once believed in them, it had always seemed to him that he was being miserably buried alive beneath them. Was it for this, God, he had wondered, that You created this glorious world, this sun, these stars, this moon, these forests and fields—so that Your chosen people could choose some dark, cramped study house to crawl into? He knew now that this entire existence was the product of a dreary, monkish isolation from life. Every man had to have something to worship—young or old, foolish or wise, everyone worshiped something, each in his own way. Only the tragic prince had long ago ceased to live a true, a natural life, and so he had ceased to worship anything vital or whole. He had stood in one place, and his worship had stood still too. For thousands of years he had led but the shadow of a life, lost like a dreamer in yesterday's dreams . . . True, Nachman thought, his people had been lucky to have snatched from the wreckage of their world a fragment of what they had lived for when they had still been healthy and strong. This fragment, which they sifted through endlessly without ever being able to make anything new of it, had given them the strength to live on, to recall past grace, as his father had said. So when winter came, the bear curled up in his lair and licked at his paws because there was nothing to eat. You too, my people, thought Nachman, lie licking your paws in your lair. But when spring came again, the bear would come back to life and once more become—a real bear. . . .

In every age, it was true, the prince had sought to free himself of his tragic curse. Not a day had gone by in all its thousands of years of exile in which the nation hadn't desperately sought a way out of its ruins. And in every age it had used the best weapons it could find. His own father, who belonged to an age gone by, hadn't once laid down his arms in all the time that Nachman could remember. His father believed that the Redemption could be brought only by a mystic awakening, and he had spent his life seeking "to weed out the brambles and thorns that grow around the heavenly rose." Now that he had aged, he wished to pass on the standard to him, Nachman, and make him swear to continue the fight. He would always remember the morning when his father had first told him to be a soldier. . . . But in taking up the flag, he could not take his father's weapons too: these had grown rusty, they would no longer do. If his people had been able to live for thousands of years in the moldy air of the cloister, rebuilding thousands of times what had been built already so as to keep from perishing from sheer idleness and ennui—why could it not also live a new life for new things under God's glorious skies? Had it not stood long enough before its ruins? It was time to move on.

To move on! But whither?

". . . sit no longer, listen to me and pass on," the cantor concluded. It was getting light out. The congregation began the morning prayer.

On the Sabbath of Consolation, the Saturday after the Ninth of Av, the entire town turned out to celebrate the marriage of Nachman, the rabbi's son, to the daughter of a wealthy Jew from a city in the province of B.

A new stream of memories flowed through his mind.

Pleasant though they were, he sought to hurry over them. It made him laugh at himself to think how he could have ever valued such baubles so greatly. He who was then so fiery of spirit, so tempestuous of soul, so quick to eye all the pettiness around him with contempt—how had he ever been transformed into the docile young man who had let his world be bounded by his new bride, her parents' home, and the gold watch they had given him for a wedding gift? To think of the innocent weeks he had spent in the company of these guileless souls, contentedly gaping at everything that should have been anathema to his spirit!

He didn't care to linger on these memories, yet in spite of himself they passed before him in a disorderly jumble that he couldn't help but enjoy. He had to smile. . . . Here, right before him, the wedding band sat in a corner and struck up a lusty tune that made the whole house shake. The jester impartially paid out his jibes to the family and its distinguished guests. A great swarm of men, women, and children in their Sabbath best and young ladies in all manner of finery ran back and forth in noisy confusion. On a chair at the far end of the hall sat a girl behind a veil. This was his bride, his beloved . . . and he truly believed that he loved her! He wanted to go over to her, to hug her and kiss her with a youthful passion . . . Now the town rabbi sat on his right and sought to engage him in a talmudic discussion. His good, simple father-in-law in a silk suit and his mother-in-law in innumerable gold trinkets circulated among the gathering in high spirits. What fools to be so merry! Could it be that they didn't know what manner of goods they were getting? Ah, how treacherous he was! The girl seemed so innocent. So did they all. He felt that he boded disaster for all of them. What kind of groom would he make? What kind of husband? He didn't want to be who they wanted him to. And yet how much like them he would have liked to be! It was so pleasant to be so untroubled. And how pretty, how lovely, this innocent girl was—what happiness it would be simply to be able to love her and be loved in return!

Just then, he remembered, his father approached him and took him aside.

"Nachman!"

"What?"

"Do you know what this evening means to you?"

"Yes, papa."

"I know that you know. You fasted and read in the holy books today, and I'm sure that you humbled yourself before God. But I want to remind you that after tonight you'll no longer be under my tutelage or my eye. You'll be going to live with your father-in-law and with the woman whom I chose for you. The girl is attractive and her parents are wealthy. Make sure, my son, that you don't become enticed by the vanity of worldly things. Make yourself holy in all that you can, because you are holy to the God of Israel. The Evil Urge grows stronger every day because of our sins, and its power to lure us from our Creator is great. So you be strong too, son, and be a man. Don't let the Evil Urge lull you to sleep. Remember that all these things, all creature comforts, are meaningless luxuries beside being a Jew. Always remember your God, Nachman!"

The wedding days came to an end. His father returned to his town. The noise and excitement was over, and Nachman was left in the home of his bride. It was an unaffected, happy, loving house. His wife was her parents' only child, their pride and their joy. For the first time Nachman realized that there were pure, unassuming, affectionate people in the world who did not ponder everything to the nth degree and sensed not the slightest tremor, not the most distant sound of battle, in their souls. Indeed, these kind, simple folk thought as little as they had to and considered everything in the best possible light. They were fearful of sin, gave alms to the poor, prayed with devotion, and dealt honestly in business, as they did with Nachman himself, whom they had purchased with good dowry money to intercede for them with his learning and help gain them a place in the world to come. And yet they let the Evil Urge lie and did not declare a private war on it like his father. The first days after his wedding were like a holiday for him, like vacations from the heder when he had been a small boy. Wherever he looked, he saw nothing but an innocent, happy tranquillity. Every corner of the house, every chair and household object seemed so quiet and peaceful. It made him feel like a boy again, and sometimes he was flooded with longing for the little stream and the craggy ledge on which he had played as a child. Once more he felt drawn to the stories in the Bible and the legends in the Midrash. With his wife he spoke little, for she was terribly shy. Yet who could have rendered into plain speech the glances that stole between them? They were brighter than summer sunlight. Each was a fiery stream, laden with longing and love; sudden, like a lightning flash in the night; and quick to disappear, leaving only a blush of shame on the cheek behind it. . . . Sometimes they would begin to stammer to each other in broken sentences and to say the simplest, the most innocent things. Then he lovingly watched her pretty lips move as she spoke, and every word seemed to his smitten soul like a holy, an angelic song. Then he raised life's cup and drank it to the full. . . .

As though on purpose, he forgot his father's parting words and erased them from his mind. Forgotten too were his "accursed philosophy" and all the thoughts and books with which he had concerned himself before the wedding. His soul softened and little by little a naive faith began to sprout within him. He felt ashamed of his ill nature that had led him to deny God His prayerful due and to lead such an empty life. Ah! What would his innocent bride and her parents think if they were to know that he was a terrible, a dangerous creature who lived without praying and even without God? He did not wish to rethink everything from the beginning; he was not really seeking to find God again; and yet without paying it much attention, he had begun to say his prayers once more. All he knew was that the simple happiness he had found in his new home demanded that he pray and refrain from thinking too much, that he make his peace with God and man. . . . And yet at the same time, he was obsessed by the bitter feeling that the situation could not long continue as it was. Something told him that he would yet be a calamity for the dwellers of this house. He would never, he was certain, be able to live out his life in peace among such people. Sooner or later a storm would blow up that would capsize everything. The dreadful thought haunted him. The more kindly his father-in-law spoke to him, the more attentively his mother-in-law cared for him, with each look his beloved wife cast at him, the more burdened, the more anxious he became . . . ah, how like a traitor he then seemed to himself!

And then his life took a new turn. His innocent wife decided to "educate" him and hired a private tutor to instruct him in the languages of the gentiles. This tutor came secretly to his room every day while his bride's parents were engaged in their business, and within a short time succeeded in teaching him to read and understand both Russian and German.

A new world was opened to him. The books of the great minds in which he now immersed himself behind the closed doors of his room worked a revolution in his entire being. The Talmud and its commentaries, the medieval Jewish philosophers of Spain and France, the various compilations of Codes, the old study house with its books—all now perished inside him. In their place lived Spinoza, Kant, Darwin, Buckle, and Spenser. Their books held him spellbound. He thought and lived nothing else.

He felt that everything that had ever mattered to him until now—all his thoughts, the very processes by which he had arrived at them—had been uprooted. He now found himself thinking along completely new lines and dreaming of new worlds which swayed him with powerful emotions. Everything was so different, so foreign: nowhere in this new frame of reference was there room for a single talmudic idea, a single passage from the cabala, a single saying taken from the old study house. He felt like a newborn babe, and his inner struggles, too, were totally new. None of the great minds to whom he now attached himself had the slightest use for the world of the Jew, about which they knew nothing, much less cared to dispute. How alike Maimonides and Levi ben Gerson, despite all the differences, now seemed to the generations of Jews who preceded them. In reading their works he had always been conscious of a struggle between closely linked worlds. But with Darwin or Buckle—there was simply no connection at all. How could he have suddenly grown so indifferent to the studies and conundrums that had occupied him in the past? Then he had lived the study house and its books; all his visions and revelations of life had sprung from this source. But now? Could he really have forgotten everything—he who had been destined to be a great rabbi in Israel? No, he could not have. He remembered after all, he had forgotten nothing. It had simply been laid away in a corner, buried in some archive of his mind. And how rich this

buried treasure was! It represented the fruits of his
mental labors over many years, the fruits of the labors of his father and his forefathers, the fruits of the
labors of his people for millennia . . . and all this he
had now swept into some corner! He was murdering
everything inside him: himself, his father, his father's
fathers, his entire people. . . .

And yet was he really? This too wasn't so. He had
found them already dead. What crime was it of his if
he had suddenly come on everything that was most
dear to him lying lifeless at his feet? The new books
had dispatched the old without his even having been
aware of the battle between them. Death was a natural law. Who was he to fight against the laws of nature? He had felt this death, this stagnation, from his
first day in the study house—and now he was free at
last. . . . He thought of his reveries about the tragic
prince. Even then he had been conscious of the
tragedy, the deathly stagnation. Even then he had
felt how the prince had stood in a trance for thousands of years and done nothing but mark time on
the same dismal spot. Even then he had realized that
the study house was the prison of an entire nation
and all its books mere prisoners' work. Even then he
had cried the great cry: enough of all this; let's move
on! And now he was actually free. He had escaped
from his cell, he had picked up his legs and moved
on—what more did he want? He had wanted to live,
to be free, to flee the dank grave, to cease playing the
tragic prince—and he had done all these things.
What more did he want? Why must he feel so sorry
for the death of the old? Why must he be so tormented by feelings of guilt?

But no, he was truly a traitor! He had not moved

on at all. Rather he had fled, more like a deserter than a general in command of his troops. And the troops had remained camped in the same place as always, in the same dismal corner, still stooped beneath the same wrathful curse. No, he hadn't freed himself from anything. He had simply gone from the camp of the vanquished to that of the victors. He, who was born poor in his father's house and suffered from want and from need along with his brothers, had deserted them now for the cozy contentment of a wealthy man's home. There he had blithely forgotten them and the ramshackle hovels in which they were wretchedly wasting away. Yes, here he was enjoying the wholesome, the handsome life of the rich, pretending to be free . . . but no, this was not freedom! The hovel was still his own; the sallow, sullen face in the doorway was still a brother's; the rickety objects inside belonged to him too. It was this new and magnificent home into which he had fallen which was still really strange to him. He had not solved anything, after all. He had simply forgotten, expunged what had once mattered to him most. What would his poor, unhappy father say? His father had told him that he must carry on his ancestors' thoughts, that the boys in the government schools were nourished by the *klipa*. Now those thoughts would go no further—the river of the past would trickle out in him too. . . .

His tutor scolded him for his "boorishness," though in reality he knew much more than him and was already far better educated. Nor was it only his tutor—all his modern young acquaintances looked down upon him as though he were a barbarian. And why? Because he still clung to the ancient badge of his people, whose customs he continued to keep and whose language he spoke. His tutor had long ago exchanged both, which meant he was "cultured" . . . Yes, just as there were those who reviled the poor not because they were ignorant but because they were poor, so the anti-Semites would always abuse the Jew not because he was less advanced than other people but because he refused to be like them. But just as no soul could manifest itself without a body, so every culture had to appear in a particular people. Everything must have a form, and it was the nation that gave its own stamp to the children of its imagination. The food of culture was universal, but every people was an organism that digested this food in its own way and turned it into living tissue. Spinoza, for instance, had been a proper Jewish dish; but because he too had felt the curse of the study house and had deserted it, it was another stomach that digested him in the end. . . . Ah, ye wretched people! At a time that a free spirit of his nation like Immanuel Kant was casting his light on the world with *A Critique of Pure Reason,* your great minds, your lovers of wisdom and science, were sitting in the impenetrable dark of the study house, reworking the same plot of ground! How intolerably bitter such a destiny was! The best of the nation's loyal sons still sat in its dreary corner and shared its curse, while those who had broken away had failed to lead a following after them from darkness to light or to rebuild the ruined hovel. Like thieves in the night, they had slipped off into a world that they had never made. . . .

No, this was not the way. His new studies had

made him fully cognizant of what he had previously only felt. He now saw with lucid eyes how there was a cosmic design to all things; he saw how nothing was random or irregular in the world, how nothing emerged out of nowhere in an already perfected state; he saw how there was nothing that didn't have its proper, its natural place, and how everything evolved in its own way and grew from its root; he saw how all human history was a burnished looking glass of peoples and gods; he saw how the great wall of human civilization had been built stone by stone and age after age; he saw the great harvests, the fruits of the imaginations of each single nation, each with its rightful place among humanity's ranks. . . .—Yes, he thought, I'll return to my people; I'll lead them and go at their head. I can't sit here any longer when my brothers are waiting. My father made me swear to be a soldier, and I will be, but not one who is detailed to guard ruins!—It was bad to mark time forever in one place, but it was no better to flee one's own hovel for another man's home. Let the people march on with its natural strength and again take its place among humanity's ranks. . . .

To march on! But whither?

A few days later he returned to his native town.

It was early in Elul, the month of repentance that precedes the High Holy Days. The summer days were still fiercely hot, but the nights were pleasant and cool, and toward morning there was already a touch of winter in the air. The little village, his father's low, cramped home, the stillness and the poverty everywhere, all made him musingly sad. For two years he had resided in a large, handsome house in a great, busy, prosperous city. He had seen the insides of a synagogue only on Sabbaths, while the rest of the week he had been free to do as he pleased, for his wife's parents were occupied with their business, and she, his beloved, indulged his every wish. It had thrilled her no end to see her husband, the young rabbi, reading and conversing in Russian with his cultivated tutor. Yet now, against her and her parents' wishes, he had taken his leave of them. His uneventful life with them had become unbearable. The house itself had begun to seem a prison to him, and its inhabitants—his warders. It had made him feel ashamed of himself.—What am I doing here? he had wondered. What good will I be to myself, what good will I be to anyone, if I stay here forever, as slothful as a frog in a stagnant pond? All my life I've thought of my people, all my life I've trained to be a soldier in command of his troops—and now I've turned into just another ten o'clock scholar! No, this isn't the place for me. Comfort can't lull a soldier like me to sleep any longer!—It was with thoughts such as these that he returned to his father's house. . . .

It was a chilly morning. A thin mist filled the air. The roads were already strewn with fallen leaves and the fields stood bared of their summer garb. The thrush no longer sang its merry song, and in its place the frogs now croaked in the ponds. He remembered the rapture he had felt one spring day while passing through this very place . . . how sad the forest now seemed! Every tree and shrub stood hunched and stricken in its misty veil, as though overcome with grief at the sight of the fields that were dying away with the summer.

The wagon slowly entered the town, whose low,

tumbledown houses with their bedraggled thatch roofs revealed themselves one by one. Human figures moved through the mist. In their pinched, hardened faces and their bodies shrunken with cold he recognized the village burghers. Now the marketplace stood before him. Women clothed in rags ran noisily hunting for bargains from stand to stand. The synagogue came into view on the far corner of the square. The streets were crowded with children on their way to the heder and with men and boys off to the morning prayer. Off in the distance he heard the bleat of the ram's horn. The Daughter of Israel was seeking the arms of her beloved, the Holy One Blessed Be He! The poor, suffering, castaway Daughter of Israel, spattered with the mire and grime of the streets, hungry for bread and thirsty for life and for air, this sickly, bone-weary maiden dressed in tatters and wrinkled from poverty and premature old age— was clinging to her lover, the Holy One Blessed Be He, while her ill, aching heart beat wildly with terror and fear! Ah, what a poor, what a pitiful thing!

A powerful sadness oppressed him. What a bleak, miserable sight! The whole town seemed to him like one large graveyard. Its houses were tombstones and its people walking shades. Death, stagnation, putrefaction . . . wherever he turned, the scent of something rotting reached his nose . . . it was the scent of death, the smell of the dead bones that lay scattered here in the valley, in this unreal, transmuted world. The accursed prisoner wished to cast off his chains; he blew the ram's horn and wrestled with the devil . . . ah, how dreadful was this world under spell!—Why, he now wondered, did I ever

part from the living to return here among the dead?
I wanted to help—but how? With what?—Even here,
in this forsaken village, the young men deserted and
made off when they could, while the nation as a
whole remained where it was. The walls of the study
house had collapsed, yet the nation refused to budge
from its corner beneath God's vast heavens. How
tragic the prisoner who remained in his dungeon
after the prison walls had tumbled, not knowing
which way to turn!

Now that he was home again, he resolved to go
among the people, to return to the old study house
and see what was uppermost on their minds. Only a
few years before he himself had still lived in this
place surrounded by ghosts. Whatever he knew then
he owed to men who had died long ago; the very air
that he breathed had been centuries old. Yet in the
end all the philosophy of a Maimonides, the astronomy of an Ibn Ezra, the primitive science of the
Tsel Olam, had not been enough for him. Now he
had begun to live in the present and to feel the pulse
of the times. Could it be, he wondered, that the Jewish people was really already dead? What had it had
to show for itself in all the hundreds of years since
these books had been written? Was what he had left
behind in the study house really the Jew's last word?
What had the nation accomplished that was new in
even the last hundred years? He wasn't asking too
much. He knew full well that no prisoner with his
hands bound in the stale air of solitary confinement
could possibly achieve what others had amid the
clean, healthy breezes of freedom. But all the same
—wherever were the ongoing thought, the mental

struggle, the wars of opinion, alas, even the dark shadows thrown by modern life?

He had long known of course that there were secular Hebrew writings, Haskalah books, as they were called, which a few young men and freethinkers had begun to read. He too had looked into such books on occasion, yet he had found them devoid of anything but empty, meaningless phrases. Was it in tracts such as these that he was expected to find the answers to his questions? Could these innocent prophecies of springtime and summer sunshine bring the nation back to life? Ah, wherever he looked he saw only death and stagnation, a black wasteland without a single ray of light to illumine his path. But he was resolved to plunge into this darkness and press on. He was a soldier and must fight! And so he made up his mind to read these new books and to befriend the young men who espoused them and who were persecuted everywhere by the old believers and reviled as profaners of the holy and as enemies of the faith. Who was to say after all that they did not really bring a breath of fresh air into the dark crannies of the Jewish soul?

That same day Nachman secretly contacted his boyhood friend Yehezkel, who was now known as one of the freethinkers.

Yehezkel was a short, slim young man with an attractively round though pasty white face, large dark eyes, and a permanent stoop that made it seem as though he were bent all the time beneath the weight of some heavy load.

"What can I do for you, Nachman?"

"I hear you read secular books, Yehezkel," said Nachman after a pause.

"So I do. But what of it?"

"I want you to lend me a few."

"You?" A look of surprise crossed Yehezkel's face.

"Yes. But no one must know."

"But what do you want with them?"

"What do I want with them? What do you want with them?"

"Me? You've asked a difficult question, one that I too ask myself all the time. I don't mean to say that I wonder why I need such books now. I need them as much as I need the air that I breathe. What I do ask myself, though, is whatever brought me to this, whatever made me want to read them in the first place."

"Tell me. I'd like to know too."

"I can't tell you anything out of the ordinary, or even terribly clear. Perhaps you'll even laugh at me, but I'll try. When I was fifteen years old I was sent to a yeshivah in Lithuania by my father, who was aware of the poor state of studies here and wanted me to become a rabbi. It's too much for me to tell you about the yeshivah and its pupils, but here, right here"—he pressed his hand over his heart—"there's still a dark corner where all the sunless years that I spent there and everything that happened in them are buried. The rabbis once said that 'the Torah is only for those who are ready to die for it,' and I was too full of life then to want to die so young. To this day I don't know exactly why it seemed to me that I was being buried alive there, but that was what I felt. . . . I didn't really know what I wanted, but I knew that something was missing. And so I began to look for it without knowing what I was looking for. I felt a weight on my mind all the time, and a great longing for something inside me. . . . My surroundings were terribly confining. The mental nourishment on which I had to subsist was pitifully little. I snatched up every new book that found its way into the yeshivah, like a sick man who can't stand the sight of food yet throws himself on every new dish that is put before him. And then by chance I came across a volume of the poetry of Adam Hacohen, and it caught my attention. The language was so beautiful, and the logic of it so true and fine, that I was terribly excited. In the same way that I hadn't known before what it was that I was missing, so now I didn't know what it was that I had found, but somehow I felt that I had found the very thing I had been looking for. From then on I began to read all the new books I could lay my hands on."

"And what did you find in them?"

"I've already said that I can't be very clear. All I can say is, see for yourself. Read a few, and if you're sensitive, you'll feel the same way as I did."

"But I already have read a few, and I haven't found a thing in them. Here you have a great, tragic people, living in exile for two thousand years—and all they have to say to it is that if only it would eat peas on Passover and stop believing in the existence of angels and devils, all would be well!"

"Ah, Nachman, Nachman, you're mistaken. It's not peas on Passover that they're offering it, but the gift of life itself; not the denial of angels and devils, but the abandonment of all its superstitions and quackeries and belief in all kinds of magic. I've already said to you that I can't be very clear, and perhaps these books aren't either, but if one thing is certain it's that the authors of them have done an enormous amount to cure our people of what ails it. They've written beautiful poems so as to give it a new, living heart; they've fought the rabbis, the leaders of the congregations, the obscurantists, the hypocrites, the yeshivahs and their deans. They've fought your death and stagnation wherever they've found it. . . ."

"But why have you stayed, then? Why remain a hated freethinker among this army of the dead when you easily could have gotten up and left?"

"You mean converted?"

"No. Simply left, once and for all. The way all the young modernizers have."

"Yes, now I understand your question. It's not easy for me to answer it. Why should I deny it? This same question has been torturing me for years. It's made me wretched, a lost spirit; it's doubled my back and killed me body and soul. Yes, I have wanted to leave. I've wanted to leave every day. I've lost the old world without gaining a new one in its place, and I've been looking for one ever since. More than once I've stood on the threshold, ready to go, and yet in the end I've always stayed put. I can't be any clearer about it, and perhaps you'll think that it's simply laziness, or that I didn't have the strength—but no, Nachman, no! I could have done it, except . . . except that I couldn't have. I myself don't know why. Something kept me here. It seemed to me that I should help change the old world rather than exchange it for something else. And the new world that tempted me was also so foreign. I felt that it wasn't for it that I had abandoned the old. And so I've remained a lost soul, a miserable freethinker adrift on life's path . . ."

"But what are you doing now?"

"I'm not doing anything. I'm standing at the crossroads without knowing which way to turn."

"And your Hebrew literature, what is it doing?"

"I tell you, I can't say anything definite. It seems to me that it too is still standing on the threshold and casting about between life and death like myself. It too has lost the old world without knowing what comes next."

"I can see my father coming. We'll have to stop now. I'll contact you secretly again, and you'll give me whatever books you have."

The wrathful days of Elul passed one by one. The Day of Atonement was already at hand. Yet Nachman couldn't forget his talk with Yehezkel. The unhappy freethinker had plunged him into a profound gloom. They were all lost, he thought to himself that night in the synagogue, every one of the miserable souls who sought to remove the ancient curse. He understood only too well all of Yehezkel's "unclear" thoughts. In his own naive way, the poor fellow was reacting directly to the realities he saw. He had spent all his time reading books that fancied themselves the "new literature"—except that there was nothing new in them, no road to take. . . . Yes, as a patient tossed and groaned in bed whenever it hurt him, and the more it hurt the more he tossed and groaned, so this "new literature" was simply the Jewish tossings and groanings of the nineteenth century, just as the cabala and Hasidism were the tossings and groanings of the Middle Ages. An entire sick nation tossing and groaning for thousands of years—each bitter groan a new variation on an age-old theme! The "new litera-ture" was like a bucketful of fish in rancid water: the fish darted this way and that, they twisted and squirmed and poked their heads above water to look for the air that they lacked . . . so Hebrew literature twisted and squirmed too: at times it too thought that the only way out lay in total assimilation, but like Yehezkel it also knew that this was impossible. . . .

Whither? Whither? Ah, whither?

It was then that the young student approached him and aroused him from his bitter thoughts. Removing his prayer shawl from over his head, he stared at the questioner with a distracted glance.

It was then that he committed the awful act of sacrilege on that awful night. . . .

Month pursued month, year followed year, and crazy Nachman sat stock-still in the synagogue, or in his room in his father's house, saying nothing. Books were his only company. Indeed, it was said that in the privacy of his room he read forbidden books too, in all kinds of languages, which were sent him by his sorrowful wife. She did not wish to grant him a di-vorce, and several times a year she came to visit him. Then Nachman broke his silence and talked, yes, talked a great deal. She wept and sighed, reasoned and implored, while he, the miserable madman, stood wretchedly before her and sighed sporadically himself, his face furrowed with despair. How greatly he suffered at such moments!

In the study house he sat by himself, quietly thinking or reviewing some text. Sometimes his father or another devotee of the Law would ask him to explain some difficult passage, which he would proceed to do, answering all their questions. But that was the extent of his sociability.

His fellow townsman remembered the curse of the Rabbi of Chernobyl. "Their bite is as the snake's and their sting as the scorpion's," they sadly whispered, recalling what was said in the Mishnah about the powers of the saints. They looked with pity at the madman, about whom all kinds of stories were told. Yet no one treated him unkindly.

And then news reached the village that caused a furor in the study house. It was clear that the madman was following it with absorption. One could tell from his face that he was sometimes gladdened and sometimes saddened by what he heard. It was as if a lightning bolt had struck his saturnine mind and filled it with a flash of new hope. He began to lend an ear to the conversations in the study house, and sometimes he joined in them himself, his voice brimming with excitement. Then the irritable expression vanished from his face, and a smile might even steal over it. . . . Sometimes too, he could be seen pacing back and forth between the walls of the study house deep in thought, his dark eyes aglow with animation, alternately knitting and relaxing his brows and gesturing with his hands and lips as though debating with someone.

A new movement was abroad in the Jewish world. The people had finally sounded the clarion call which he himself had heard long ago: to march on! But the people was not asking whither. It already knew where. To the land of its fathers! Yes, whenever two Jews were seen talking in those days, it was bound to be about Palestine. . . . In its innocence, the people had even begun to tell all kinds of miraculous stories about the "redemption of the land" by Jewish heroes and the mass return there that would soon commence, while it dreamt of the new life that awaited it in its ancient homeland, where every man would peacefully recline "under his fig tree and under his vine." Permission was even given to bring Zionist literature into the study house, from which the townsmen slaked their great thirst for news of what was happening in the privy chambers where its great leaders were laboring to end its long exile. Crazy Nachman too was among the readers of these publications, and he perused every line of the lengthy arguments for the profitability of colonizing the Holy Land. Often, however, he would frown after reading them, for the thing he was looking for was not to be found there. . . .

—Ah, unhappy people, he then thought. So accustomed had it become to its life of slavery and degradation, to its little plot of swamp-ridden ground, that it no longer even felt the wrath of God upon it. Its tragedy was that even now it did not really wish to remove the ancient curse, to cast off its chains and emerge from its prison into the light of day to live a rich, productive life. If the accursed prisoner was trying at all to leave his dungeon even now, it was only because others were driving him out. . . . so that once again the people of Exile stood with its pack on its back, looking to find a new little plot where it might again fend hunger from the door. How pathetic were the hopes of a people that could not even for a moment rise above thoughts of its stomach! True, when he had first heard the summons to Palestine, he felt as though he had been freshly reborn. His consciousness had seemed to expand and a stream of new thoughts had coursed busily through it. It was as if a revolution in his being had made happiness of all his despair. Over what, he then asked himself, had he been suffering all these years? What need had there been for his madness, his isolation from life, when there was so much to do, so much new movement and light? If the Jewish people had never forgotten its homeland in all its years of bitter exile, how could he, who fancied himself its general, have done such a thing? Yet had he really? No, he felt as though the sacred "If I forget thee, O Jerusalem" had always been inscribed in his heart. He hadn't forgotten at all; he had always remembered; he just hadn't known the way. . . . He had lost the faith that people and land could be redeemed through prayer and meditation; he had seen his people in its poverty, in its trials and tribulations, in its dishonor and humiliation; wherever he had looked, wherever he had turned, there it had been, a fallen giant . . . a tragic prince. Yes, wherever he had seen the Jew's ancient grandeur, he had seen his dishonor and his curse as well. He had realized then that his people's wound was as vast as the sea, that it went very deep and was very old, yet he had known of nothing that might heal it. . . . But now that the people had awakened, and was seeking to find its way home not through mysticism or magic, but through hard work, education, and reform, had it not rid itself of its curse once and for all? Ah, if only it were so! But the tragic prince was still unaware of his tragedy; he no longer even knew he was a prince or that it was beneath him to wallow on the muddy ground. . . . Yes, the people's heart had grown musty and stale; it no longer wanted a life of freedom and work but simply a crust of bread and rest for its weary bones. The Israelites who had marched forth from Egypt had brought the Law with them to the promised land, the exiles returning from Babylon a purified faith—each had brought something of its own, each had returned healthy and whole to worship a God not worshipable elsewhere among the deities and customs of the nations. And now? Now the people sought to come home simply as a slave fleeing before hunger and the whip. It could never be healed in this way or its curse removed. It must not return to its homeland an ailing and broken invalid to live the life of exile all over again. The Hebrew race must come home to lay the basis of a new way of life—to exist not as the degenerate social body that it presently was but as one that was vibrant, healthy and alive—a society that would again be an example to the entire world as once the ancient Hebrew civilization had been, that would bring new life, new hope, and a new awakening . . .

The excitement over the new movement grew in the village, and one winter evening a grand meeting was called of all the youth. The assembly was tumultuous. Several young men rose to speak heatedly about the dangers of anti-Semitism and the need to settle in Palestine. Suddenly crazy Nachman appeared among the gathering. To the amazement of all, he strode to the front of the hall and requested permission to speak.

The unexpected drama took the audience by surprise. Fear and consternation were on everyone's face. It was possible to hear a pin drop. The madman stood by the speaker's stand and began:

"Dear brothers! Please allow me to say a few things to you tonight. Afterwards you can laugh as you like, but hear me out first. The situation of my people, my desire to help it, and my inability to do anything for it have driven me mad. I've stood at a distance from life because life had no place for me. You, my brothers, may have sympathized, but none of you have ever understood me. My heart is a tinder-box, and if ever I had wanted to open it for you, you would have seen the fireworks inside . . . except that this was always impossible. What I say to you tonight will be brief, because it would take me many months and years to unburden myself before you completely. Yes, all these years I've never stopped thinking, and to make you truly understand I would have to tell you all these thoughts, but this simply isn't possible. . . .

"You, my brothers," Nachman continued after a brief pause, "are gathered here tonight to seek a cure for our people's illness and to help restore it to its ancient homeland. I can see by your faces that you think of yourselves as national heroes and look with a smile of contempt upon all the generations before you who did nothing for our people. But this is a grave mistake. Every person thinks he is a world in himself, and every age is convinced that it is the salt of the earth and the last word in human perfection. But history is an impartial judge: it counts the years by the thousands, and a generation here or there is merely a grain of sand in its eyes! I haven't come here tonight to discuss the great movement that you are part of, because many have spoken about it already and it would again take me many days to tell you all that is on my mind. And yet nevertheless, I would like to share a few general thoughts with you. . . .

"The Jewish people," Nachman continued after another pause in a more powerful voice, "has always taken part in whatever great movements were sweeping the world at the time. The oldest records demonstrate that in their earliest prehistory the Hebrews wandered nomadically together with many other great tribes. Every great period in Jewish history has been a great period in the history of mankind as well; every period of displacement and exile has involved the displacement and exile of stronger nations too. When the Jews went forth from Egypt to seek a new homeland in Asia, there was a mighty migration of peoples all through the African continent, and by the same token, when we were exiled by the Assyrians and the Babylonians, many other peoples were driven from their homelands too, and the whole earth was in turmoil. . . . Or to come closer to our own age, consider the Roman Empire. It was then that the West took its place in the sun and the East lapsed into its night of decline. (Of course, it was the Greeks who first caused the demise of the East, on the ruins of which the West was built.) Along with the rest of the East fell that people of the East—the Judeans. And yet the truth of the matter is that this whole great cataclysm was more spiritual than military. When a large body of air is evenly heated it drifts slowly and quietly along, but when a cold front meets a hot front terrible storms are created that can wreak untold havoc. And if one looks carefully at the history of the world, one sees that all the great movements in human life have been basically those of the spirit. The human race can't live without ideals, and so it brings forth its great men, its prophets, and its lawgivers to create something for it to worship. Yet none of these ideals lasts forever. Of course, the more penetratingly the prophet looks into the crystal ball of the future, the stronger and more long-lasting is the ideal that he creates, the more hundreds or thousands of years it will survive; but sooner or later its time too must come. Suddenly humanity feels that everything is empty and rotten and that life has no meaning anymore. Such ages are the most dreadful of all, the whole world then thirsts for the word of God . . . nations disintegrate into parties and factions, each searching for its own private truth . . . but this situation too cannot last forever. Eventually humanity finds its new prophet, who gives it a new god and a new civilization that is built on the bones of the old. Then great movements sweep the globe and humanity expels from its midst whatever is degenerate and rotten and spawns the elements of a new, healthy life from amid the ruins and the graveyards. Such was the age in which our Second Temple was destroyed, from about a century and a half before the destruction to about two centuries after. Then all the gods of the pagan world languished and declined; the human race felt weary and exhausted; every man sought his own revelation; the old civilizations crumbled and collapsed; the religions of the East were discarded and the peoples sought another faith. Then the West built a new civilization on the foundations of the East, of Judaism. . . .

"I'm not a teller of fortunes, and I don't want to repeat things to you that have already been said by others. I simply want to say that the age in which we now live resembles this previous age in every respect. Europe is ailing now—everyone feels how our civilization is coming apart and how its pillars of faith are already eaten through. Society is weary of it all and thirsts once again for a new word of God, for the prophet and the lawgiver. The minor prophets now appearing in its midst can extend its lease on life only temporarily. Kant gave it a reprieve of a century; Darwin too may occupy it for as long. But the great prophet and lawgiver who will bring the word to the weary and enable the world to move onward has yet to appear, and meanwhile humanity must wander in the dark until a new wind blows from God and brings it the nourishment on which to live for another thousand years. . . .

"And here I want to say to you, my brothers, that not only are we ourselves eastward bound, but that the whole West has been journeying in this direction for some time. . . . I myself—you may laugh if you wish—am convinced that the day is not far off when those dry bones, the hundreds of millions of citizens of the East, will come to life and create new, vital nations that will found an entirely new civilization. Then the East will bestir itself and rule over the fallen West, just as the West ruled the world after the downfall of the East. And you, my brothers, in your eastward journey, must always remember that you are Easterners by birth. At a time when the entire

West is turning eastward to plunder the dead, it is you who must go there to revive them and to take part in the construction of the civilization that is to come. The greatest enemy that Judaism has ever had has been . . . the West, which is why I believe it to be unnatural that we Hebrews, we Easterners, should throw in our lot with the West as we set out for the East. I believe that the Hebrew nation will live and stand on its feet; I believe that this great people, without whose books and spiritual genius the world could not possibly have achieved what it has, will again give a new civilization to the human race; but this civilization will be Eastern. The great East will revive from its slumber and return to the natural life, and the accursed people will march at its head, at the head of the living East. . . .

"And so, my brothers, in journeying eastward, do not go as enemies of the East but as its admirers and loyal sons. Make sure you are bringing it life and not death. Millennia have elapsed from the days of the prophet Balaam until now, and still we feel that we are only in the middle of the way and that we must say about ourselves as he did: 'I see him, but not now; I behold him, but not nigh.' I was driven mad because I didn't know where to turn or how to escape, and now it's too late for me to change. There were days when I thought that I myself would stand in the vanguard of my people, but I now know that this cannot be. Let a new generation go before the people. And if the Jewish people has a destiny to fulfill, let it forge that destiny and that truth for itself and take them with it to the East. Not just to Palestine but to the entire East . . . only then can it know that it has taken the right and the natural path! And finally, my brothers, let none of you have the presumption to think that your generation can finish the task by itself. Let it be written on your banners: 'I see him, but not now; I behold him, but not nigh.' To the East! To the East!"

There was a sudden stirring among the audience. One of the young men loudly interrupted the speaker. The madman, however, did not seem to mind, nor did he wait to find out how his remarks had been received. Beads of perspiration fell on his flushed face, which was then remarkably handsome. Without another word, he walked out and went home.

The grand meetings were over, their participants long gone. The "colonization of Palestine" was a thing of the past for the inhabitants of the little village, who once had dreamed of being there soon, each man under his fig tree and under his vine. Life went its usual way, changing everything in its path. Only the madman still sat on as before in his dusky corner, silent and alone, speaking to no one and answering no one's questions. His face had grown lined and his burning eyes had receded deep into their sockets. His hair and beard were matted and thick, his clothing threadbare and torn. One look at him was enough to know that he was mad.

His speech at the meeting hall was the last outward spark he threw off. From then on God's candle burned gradually down within him, until death had compassion and snuffed out his tedious life.

Glossary

The glossary that follows contains brief explanations of words, names, and customs mentioned in the text that are likely to be unfamiliar to the general reader. The entries are listed according to the number of the page on which they occur in the text. If an entry has occurred in a previous story, the reader is referred back to it. In each story an entry is listed only the first time it occurs.

Yankev the Watchman

page

41   Woe that the Shekhinah is in exile!:   In rabbinic legend the Shekhinah, God's indwelling presence

among men, is depicted as having gone into exile along with the people of Israel upon the destruction of the Temple.

42   a midnight vigil: It was common practice in East European pietist circles to rise in the middle of the night in order to recite psalms and pray for the Shekhinah in its exile, and for its restoration to God that will presage the coming of the Messiah.

44   the high priests of his people: The leaders of the Jewish community (see Introduction, pp. 14–15).

45   Asmodai: In rabbinic legend, king of the demons and of the demonic realm.

48   before the imperial throne: An allusion to the emancipation of the serfs by Alexander II in 1861.

49   the heder: the traditional one-room schoolhouse of the shtetl, in which Hebrew and religious subjects were taught.

The Shadows

52   the study house: The synagogue in the shtetl was commonly referred to as the *bet hamidrash,* "the study house"; here the community's religious texts were kept, which Jews would come to pore over at hours when services were not being held.

52   Talmud: The main authoritative compendium of Jewish Law, or halakhah, redacted in the sixth century C.E., consisting of thirty-six tractates of commentary upon the Mishnah (see note to p. 94).

52   the holy ark: The high wooden chest at the front of the synagogue in which the parchment scrolls of the Pentateuch are kept.

55   the day breatheth, and the shadows flee away: Song of Songs 2:17.

57 the Maharsha: Rabbi Samuel Eliezer Eidels of Lublin (1560–1631), author of a well-known talmudic commentary.

57 Alfasi: Isaac Alfasi of Fez (1013–1103), one of the foremost medieval halakhic authorities.

57 Mordecai: Mordecai ben Hillel Hacohen of Nuremberg (1240–1298), talmudic commentator.

57 Reb Asher: Asher ben Yehiel (1250–1327), author of the halakhic compendium *Piskei ha-Rosh*.

57 Maimonides: Moses ben Maimon (1135–1204), philosopher and halakhic codifier of the Spanish period, generally recognized as the greatest of medieval Jewish minds. His philosophical writings were essentially an attempt to synthesize the concepts of Aristotelianism with the beliefs and practices of Judaism.

57 the *Tur:* The *Tur Orah Hayyim*, the great legal compendium of the talmudist Jacob ben Asher (1269–1340), the son of Asher ben Yehiel.

57 Joseph Caro: Palestinian mystic and cabalist (1488–1575), whose guidebook to Jewish Law and ritual observance, the *Shulhan Arukh*, became one of the most popular and widely consulted texts of East European Jewry.

57 *The Kuzari:* A philosophical defense of Judaism, written in dialogue form, by Yehudah Halevi of Spain (1085–1140), commonly considered the greatest of medieval Hebrew poets.

57 *The Guide to the Perplexed:* The main philosophical work of Maimonides, as distinguished from *The Strong Hand*, his opus of halakhic commentary.

57 *The Beliefs and Opinions:* A philosophical exposition of Judaism by Saadia Gaon of Babylonia

(892–942), the earliest classic of medieval Jewish philosophy.

57   *The Wars of the Lord:*   A philosophical work on Judaism by Levi ben Gerson (1288–1344), philosopher, mathematician, and astronomer of the Spanish period.

57   the Evil Urge: The *yetser ha-ra*, in rabbinic literature that aspect of the human personality to which sinful and libidinous inclinations are ascribed.

57   Purim: A holiday commemorating the events of the Book of Esther, occurring in the Hebrew month of Adar, in late winter.

58   Reb Shlomo: The term *Reb*, derived from the Hebrew-Yiddish word *rebbe*, "rabbi," was a common title of respect among East European Jews.

58   *The Strong Hand:* See note to p. 57 on *The Guide to the Perplexed.*

59   The Torah: Specifically, the Pentateuch or Five Books of Moses, but in its broader sense, the entire body of Jewish sacred literature and law.

63   earlocks: The long sideburns, generally brushed back or curled behind the ears, worn by Orthodox Jewish males in fulfillment of the Mosaic injunction in Leviticus 19:27: "Ye shall not round the corners of your heads."

A Spring Night

66   Bava Kama: A talmudic tractate dealing with torts, one commonly assigned to beginning students.

66   *The Kuzari:*   See note to p. 57.

66   *Yoreh De'ah:*   One of the four sections of the

Shulḥan Arukh (see note to p. 57 on Joseph Caro).

66 *The Guide to the Perplexed:*   See note to p. 57.

66 *The Beginnings of Wisdom:*   Edifying work by the Palestinian cabalist Eliyahu de Vidas (1550–1588).

66 forbidden Hebrew books: Secular Haskalah literature (see Introduction, pp. 8–9).

67 The meadows are clothed with flocks . . . :   Psalms 65:14.

68 springs are sent forth . . . :   Psalms 104:10–11.

The Calf

73 heder: See note to p. 49.

73 the protruding fringes of his dirty undershawl: In fulfillment of the Mosaic injunction in Numbers 15:37, "Speak unto the children of Israel, and bid them that they make . . . fringes in the corners of their garments," Orthodox male Jews wear a poncho-like cloth pullover with knotted corners underneath their shirt.

74 Talmud: See note to p. 52.

74 the afternoon and evening prayer: Of the three prayer services recited by Orthodox Jews every day, the last two are generally said together, the one right before and the other right after sundown.

76 eighteen pennies: Donations to charity in the shtetl were commonly made in units of eighteen, the numerical value of the letters in the Hebrew verb *ḥai,* "to live."

76 Rabbi Meir Baal Haness: Rabbi Meir "the miracle-worker," a semilegendary second-century rabbi and "patron" of the alms box in Eastern Europe.

79   into Thy hand I commit my spirit: A verse from
     Psalms 31:6, said regularly as part of the prayer
     upon retiring at night.

In the Evening

81   the third Torah reading in the Book of Genesis:
     One of the fifty-four parshiot, or portions, into
     which the Pentateuch is divided in Jewish tradition
     is read every Sabbath around the year. The annual
     cycle begins with the holiday of *Simḥat Torah*,
     "the Rejoicing of the Law," which occurs in early
     autumn, when the first chapters of the Book of
     Genesis are read. Thus, the week of the third read-
     ing would begin two Sabbaths later.

82   the heder: See note to p. 49.

83   the afternoon and evening prayer: See note
     to p. 74.

84   the Great Synagogue: The name generally
     given to the main synagogue in those shtetls that
     had more than one.

84   the eternal light: The candle or lamp in the syna-
     gogue that is perpetually kept burning above the
     holy ark.

84   the podium: The raised platform in the center
     or front of the synagogue from which the cantor
     recites the service and from which the Torah is
     read.

84   the holy ark: See note to p. 52.

84   the Torah scrolls: The parchment scrolls of the
     Pentateuch that are kept in the holy ark.

84   Let a priest come forth for the first blessing!:
     During the weekly reading of the portion from the
     Pentateuch in the synagogue each Sabbath, eight

members of the congregation are called up at intervals to the podium to recite a blessing over the Torah and stand by the reader as he reads from the scroll. The first of these must be a Kohen, or hereditary priest, and the second a Levite, while the remaining six are drawn from the congregation at large. The eighth blessing, or maftir, is recited by the worshiper who afterward reads the weekly portion from the Prophets, the haftarah, and is a special honor commonly reserved for bar mitzvah boys, young men about to be married, etc.

84 Reb Gronim: See note to p. 58 on Reb Shlomo.

85 the final portion: The last eighth of the weekly reading from the Pentateuch.

86 golems: In Jewish medieval legend a golem was a manmade automaton, lacking powers of intelligence of its own.

87 Get thee from thy land . . . :   God's command to Abraham to leave Ur of the Chaldees and set out for Canaan (Genesis 12:1), with which the third weekly reading from Genesis begins.

88 earlocks: See note to p. 63.

88 goyim!:   Gentiles!

91 Yoske: Affectionate Yiddish form of Yosef, "Joseph."

94 the Baal Shem Tov: Israel of Medzibozh in the Ukraine (c. 1698–1760), the itinerant faith healer and wonder-worker who was the founder of the Hasidic movement.

94 a minyan: A group of ten Jews, the minimum required for the holding of public prayer.

94 The Mishnah: The basic halakhic commentary on the Bible, redacted in the third century C.E., on which the Talmud is a commentary in turn.

94   The *Zohar:*   A greatly revered thirteenth-century cabalistic text, popularly attributed to the second-century rabbi Shimon bar Yohai, which enjoyed almost canonical status among East European Jews, particularly in Hasidic circles.

95   Samael: In rabbinic literature and popular folklore, the devil or personification of evil.

95   a goy: A gentile.

95   *klipa:*   Literally, "husk"; in cabalistic theosophy, the outward, material, and sensual aspect of things, and hence, by extension, the power of evil.

95   Moshke: Yiddish diminutive of Moshe, "Moses," used by Poles as a pejorative term for a Jew.

97   all seven sciences: The seven medieval disciplines of theology, natural science, astronomy, arithmetic, geometry, music, and rhetoric.

97   *zhid:*   Polish, Russian: a Jew.

99   a Jewish boy of thirteen: The age at which a boy becomes bar mitzvah, that is, personally responsible for all the observances and rituals of Jewish Law.

100   Yiddish: The Germanic dialect spoken by the Jews of Eastern Europe, written in the Hebrew alphabet.

100   the vowels too: In Hebrew writing the vowels do not appear as letters, but are indicated by dots or lines above or below the consonants.

101   Amsterdam: A noted center of Jewish studies in the eighteenth century, especially renowned for its talmudical college, the Great or *Ets Ḥayyim* Yeshivah.

101   amulet: Among East European Jews, com-

monly a small wooden or metal container with scriptural verses or magical charms inside, or else a flat metal plate with verses inscribed on its surface.

102 How could he eat without washing?: In Orthodox ritual, eating is always preceded by the washing of hands accompanied by the appropriate blessing.

102 the *Shema:* The confession of faith beginning with the verse "Hear, O Israel [*Shema Yisra'el*], the Lord our God, the Lord is one" (Deuteronomy 6:4), which is recited daily in the morning and evening service and again upon retiring at night.

102 the thirty-six Just Souls: According to popular Jewish legend, there are in existence in every generation thirty-six perfectly just souls, on account of whose righteousness alone humanity is allowed to survive in spite of its sins.

102 the Seven Shepherds: In rabbinic legend, the biblical figures—all shepherds by vocation—of Adam, Seth, Methuselah, Abraham, Jacob, Moses, and David, based on the verse in Micah 5:4, "Then shall we raise against him seven shepherds, and eight princes among men."

103 Asmodai: See note to p. 45.

104 the unclean lizards: According to rabbinic legend, the Roman armies were aided in their destruction of the Temple by a scourge of lizards, who helped spread the fire from one part of the sanctuary to another.

104 the Evil Urge: See note to p. 57.

104 the mezuzah: A small wooden or metal case containing a parchment scroll with verses from the Bible, hung by Orthodox Jews over the doorways

of their homes in observance of the Mosaic injunction in Deuteronomy 6:9, "And thou shalt write them upon the door-posts of thy house, and upon thy gates."

The Amulet

107   for hands to be washed before prayer in the morning: An Orthodox Jew's first task upon rising is to wash his hands and recite the proper blessing over them. Only then may he say his morning prayers.

108   the *Shema:*   See note to p. 102.

109   Polonnoye: A town in the Ukraine in which some ten thousand Jews were massacred during Chmielnicki's uprising.

109   Chmielnicki: Bogdan   Chmielnicki   (1595–1657), leader of the cossack and peasant uprising in the Ukraine against the Poles in 1648–49, in the course of which tens of thousands of Jews were slaughtered and many more driven from their homes.

109   the heder: See note to p. 49.

110   the holy rabbi: The rabbi of Lyubavitch in White Russia, head of the Hasidic sect of Habad, to which Feierberg's father belonged (see introduction, p. 4).

111   *klayzl:*   Among Hasidim, a small synagogue or room used for prayer.

111   Shneur Zalman: Rabbi Shneur Zalman of Ladi (1745–1813), a disciple of the Maggid of Mezritsh (see note below) and founder of the Hasidic sect of Habad.

112   a degree: In cabalistic (see note to p. 142 on the

cabala) and Hasidic thought, a Jew was considered as having to climb a ladder of spiritual rungs or "degrees," each one of which represents a higher level of perfection.

112 the Baal Shem Tov: See note to p. 94.

112 the Maggid of Mezritsh: Rabbi Dov Baer of Mezritsh (1710–1772), an early disciple of the Baal Shem Tov and among the most revered of Hasidic holy men, or tsaddikim.

112 the Grandfather of Shpola: Rabbi Aryeh Leib of Shpola in the Ukraine (1725–1812), an early Hasidic tsaddik and popular faith healer.

112 the Old Man of Chernobyl: Rabbi Menahem Nahum Twersky (1730–1787), a disciple of the Baal Shem Tov and founder of the dynasty of Chernobyl Hasidim in the Ukraine (see introduction, p. 7).

112 *klipa:*   See note to p. 95.

112 tsaddik: In Hasidism, a rabbi or holy man who has the power of intercession between man and God.

112 a misnagid: Literally, an "opponent," the term used by the Hasidim, and eventually by their rivals as well, to refer to those Jews who remained hostile to or apart from the Hasidic movement. Although Hasidism originated in circles where cabalistic beliefs and influences were strong, there were individual cabalists and cabalistic groups that remained aloof from the movement even after it had gained a mass following.

112 the great chain: In cabalistic tradition, the authoritative line of mystic knowledge descending from Rabbi Shimon bar Yohai (see note to p. 94 on the *Zohar)* to the great Palestinian cabalist Isaac Luria (1534–1572) and his disciple Hayyim Vital (1543–1620).

113   earlocks: See note to p. 63.

114   the Shekhinah: See note to p. 41.

116   melamed: A tutor of religious subjects to children.

116   *tsitsis:*   The knotted fringes worn by Orthodox Jews (see note to p. 73).

116   mezuzahs: See note to p. 104.

117   her ten spheres: In cabalistic theosophy, ten spheres of emanated holiness separate the Godhead from the material creation and the world of man, which constitutes part of the tenth, or last, of these.

117   secular schools: The Yiddish schools opened by the Russian government in the reign of Alexander II with the object of offering the Jews of Russia a secular education and weaning them away from the traditions of Orthodoxy.

117   Samael: See note to p. 95.

117   the Evil Urge: See note to p. 57.

117   an amulet: See note to p. 101.

Whither?

122   the heder: See note to p. 49.

122   the old holy man of Chernobyl: See note to p. 112. Here, however, the reference is apparently not to Menahem Nahum, but to his grandson Aaron of Chernobyl (1787–1882), to whose Hasidic court most of the Jews of Novograd-Volinsk, though not Feierberg's father, paid allegiance.

122   Reb Moshe: See note to p. 58 on Reb Shlomo.

122   Samael: See note to p. 95.

123   the *klipa:*   See note to p. 95.

123   even though he knew that it was forbidden . . . :

In the disastrous aftermath of the seventeenth-century messianic movement led by the pretender Sabbetai Zevi, in which cabalistic influences and expectations played a dominant role, the rabbis of Eastern Europe forbade the study of cabalistic literature to anyone under the impressionable age of twenty-five, or variously thirty, years.

123 Elisha ben Avuyah: A second-century mishnaic sage and disciple of Rabbi Akiva, one of four prominent scholars of his generation, according to rabbinic tradition, to enter the "gardens" of mystical contemplation. In the end he became a heretic and renounced the practice of Judaism entirely.

123 what's above and what's below . . . :   A reference to a passage in the Talmud forbidding the study of "what is above and what is below, what is ahead and what is behind," that is, the philosophical investigation of the universe and of religious articles of faith.

124 The Day of Atonement: The fast day of Yom Kippur, occurring in the Hebrew month of Tishri, in early autumn, the holiest day of the Jewish year.

124 the ark: See note to p. 52.

124 the podium: See note to p. 84.

124 The "Song of Unity":   A mystical medieval poem about the Divinity, sung at the end of the holiday service.

125 the ritual performed by the high priest: The annual sacrificial rite of atonement performed on the Temple Mount, a detailed description of which occurs in the Yom Kippur liturgy.

126 And he picked up the candle . . . and blew it out: Among the acts strictly forbidden on Sabbaths and the major Jewish holidays, especially on the Day of

Atonement, is the lighting or extinguishing of any fire.

128   the Talmud: See note to p. 52.

128   the afternoon and evening service: See note to p. 74.

128   the Evil Urge: See note to p. 57.

129   Mishnah: See note to p. 94.

130   *The Beginnings of Wisdom:*   See note to p. 66.

131   the mezuzah: See note to p. 104.

133   the "other side": The *sitra aḥra*, in cabalistic and Hasidic terminology, the devil or kingdom of evil.

134   the midnight vigil: See note to p. 42.

134   Remember, O Lord . . . :   Lamentations 5:1.

135   O God, the heathen are come . . . :   Psalms 79: 1–2.

135   Though Thou hast crushed us . . . :   Psalms 44: 20–26.

135   I have set watchmen . . . :   Isaiah 62:6.

135   the Wailing Wall: The Western Wall of the Temple compound, the one remnant of the structure left standing after the Roman destruction of Jerusalem in 70 C.E., and the holiest of Jewish shrines.

135   a fox ran stealthily in and out of its breaches: An image taken from rabbinic legends about the ruined Temple, which are in turn based on the verse in Lamentations 5:18, "For the mountain of Zion, which is desolate; the foxes walk upon it."

135   Woe to the father . . . :   An allusion to God's exiling of the people of Israel in the talmudic tractate Berakhot.

136   King David: In rabbinic legend, King David is portrayed as haunting the ruins of Jerusalem, wait-

ing for the coming of the Messiah to free it once again or, in alternate versions, for the time when he can arise and be the Messiah himself.

136   Then Mother Rachel too: A motif in Jewish legend that has its source in Jeremiah 31:15, "A voice is heard in Ramah, lamentation, and bitter weeping, Rachel weeping for her children; she refuseth to be comforted for her children, because they are not."

136   The Shekhinah: See note to p. 41.

137   Joseph de la Reina: Fifteenth-century Palestinian cabalist and mystic, whose semilegendary life was devoted to bringing the Messiah through his own spiritual efforts.

137   The blessed Ari: Rabbi Isaac Luria (see note to p. 112 on the great chain), who lived a life fraught with messianic expectations and was rumored by his disciples to be the Messiah himself.

137   the Baal Shem Tov: See note to p. 94.

140   Arise O Edom and Ishmael . . . :   A "verse" concocted by Nachman out of various bits and snatches of the Prophets.

140   Gog and Magog: In Ezekiel 38 and 39, Gog, king of Magog, is one of the enemies of Israel on whom God's vengeance will fall at the end of days.

140   the Sons of Ammon: Like the Philistines, traditional enemies of the Israelites in the Bible.

142   the cabala: In Jewish tradition, a generic term for the corpus of medieval theosophic literature dealing with the nature of the Godhead and Its relation to Israel and to the world.

145   the *Shulḥan Arukh:*   See note to p. 57 on Joseph Caro.

146   the Holy One Blessed Be He: A common appellation of God in rabbinic literature.

146   *Likkutei Tsvi:*   An anthology of prayers for special occasions that was in widespread use among East European Jews.

146   the Days of Awe: The ten-day period of prayer and penitence starting with Rosh Hashana, the Jewish New Year, and ending with Yom Kippur, the Day of Atonement.

146   Where is the place of His glory: A line from the Kedushah or "holiness" section of the morning service (so called because it contains the verse "Holy, holy, holy is the Lord God of Hosts"), which is sung responsively by the cantor and the standing congregation.

146   the three patriarchs: Abraham, Isaac, and Jacob. According to a rabbinic legend, when Jacob sought to reveal the secret date of the coming of the Messiah to his twelve sons, God deprived him of the knowledge.

147   the ram's horn: The shofar, which is sounded daily throughout the month of Elul, the thirty-day penitential period, occurring in late summer, that precedes the Days of Awe.

147   The Lord is my light and my salvation . . . :   From Psalms 27, which is recited daily in the morning service from the start of the penitential period of Elul.

147   the holy *Shiloh:*   The *Shnei Luḥot ha-Berit* of Isaiah Halevi Horowitz (1565–1630), a cabalistic work on the subject of repentance.

148   the penitential service: Throughout the month of Elul a special service is held in the synagogue for which observant Jews rise in the middle of the night.

148   to wash his hands before sitting down to the table: See note to p. 102.

148   the ritual bath: The mikveh, or indoor pool, which was used in the shtetl for both physical cleansing and ritual purification.

148   the Kedushah prayer: See note to p. 146 on Where is the place of His glory.

149   Hoshanna Rabba: The last day of the eight-day holiday of Succot, the Feast of Tabernacles, with which the festive period ushered in by the New Year comes to a close.

151   exiles from Portugal: In 1492 the Jews were expelled from the entire Iberian Peninsula.

151   Polonnoye: See note to p. 109.

151   Kamenietz: The town of Kamenietz-Podolsk in the Ukraine, where bloody massacres of the Jews took place during the Chmielnicki uprising (see notes to p. 109).

151   the *Midrash Rabba:*   One of the main compendiums of midrashim, or rabbinic legends and homilies based on the Bible, dating from the geonic period (600–1000 C.E.).

151   the Ninth of Av: The ninth day of the Hebrew month of Av, occurring in midsummer, a fast day that commemorates the destruction of the First and Second Temples.

151   the magnificent children of Jerusalem: A legend in the *Midrash Rabba* tells of how a party of children from Jerusalem, taken captive by the Romans, chose to commit mass suicide in order to escape the ignominy of slavery and exile.

152   the *Yoreh De'ah:*   See note to p. 66.

157   For thou art a holy people . . . :   Deuteronomy 14:2.

157   Thou hast avouched the Lord this day . . . : Deuteronomy 26:17–19.

158 the Midrash: The collective corpus of midrashic anthologies (see note to p. 151 on the *Midrash Rabba*).

158 the *Yosifon:* A popular medieval history of the Jews written in Hebrew by an unknown author and based partly on the works of Josephus Flavius, whence its name.

158 the *Shevet Yehudah:* A history of Jewish persecutions written by the Spanish exile and Marrano Solomon ibn Verga (c. 1475–c. 1525).

158 the *Shalshelet ha-Kabbalah: The Chain of Tradition,* a Hebrew history written by the cabalist Gedaliah ben Yosef ibn Yahia (1515–1587).

158 the *Tsemah David:* A popular Jewish and general history written in Hebrew by David Gans of Prague (1541–1613).

159 the *Zohar:* See note to p. 94.

159 Hayyim Vital: See note to the great chain on p. 112.

159 Maimonides' *Guide:* See note to p. 57 on *The Guide to the Perplexed.*

159 *The Kuzari:* See note to p. 57.

161 Prince Don Isaac Abrabanel: Leader of the Spanish Jewish community (1437–1508) who was instrumental in rallying the Jews of Spain at the time of their expulsion in 1492 and persuading thousands of them to go into exile rather than convert to Christianity.

161 Menasseh ben Israel: Rabbi of Amsterdam and descendant of Spanish exiles (1604–1657), who engaged in numerous polemic defenses of Judaism and sought from his pulpit to secure political rights for the Jewish communities of Europe, and in par-

ticular to gain their readmittance to England, from which they had been expelled in the thirteenth century.

162   the government schools: See note to p. 117 on secular schools.

163   Bava Kama: See note to p. 66.

163   Nezikin: The section of the Talmud dealing with torts, of which Bava Kama forms the first part.

165   the story . . . in the Book of Judges: Judges 11:29–40.

165   Lag B'Omer: A minor holiday occurring in springtime, in the Hebrew month of Iyar, commemorating a victory over the Romans by Rabbi Akiva and his disciples (see note to p. 170) during the Bar Kokhba revolt (132–135 C.E.). It was celebrated in Eastern Europe mainly by the children, who were allowed to go out to the woods and play at being soldiers.

167   the *P'nei Yehoshua:*   A talmudic commentary by Yakov Yehoshua Falk (1681–1756), rabbi of Frankfurt on the Main.

167   the Maharsha: See note to p. 57.

167   the Maharram Shif: Meir ben Yakov Schiff (1605–1641), German rabbi and talmudic commentator.

167   Rashi: Rabbi Shlomo Yitzhaki of Troyes (1040–1105), author of the most popular and widely consulted of all medieval biblical and talmudic commentaries.

168   Come, my beloved . . . :   The Song of Songs 7:12–14.

168   Thus said the Daughter of Israel . . . : An allegorical homily upon the verse from The Song of Songs, taken from the talmudic tractate of Eruvin and from the *Midrash Rabba* (see note to p. 151). In

rabbinic literature the Daughter of Israel is a common personification of the Jewish people.

170   Rabbi Akiva: A second-century mishnaic sage who was tortured and killed by the Romans for his participation in the Bar Kokhba revolt.

170   Rabbi Yosi: Apparently Feierberg intended to refer not to the second-century sage Rabbi Yosi, but to his contemporary Rabbi Yehudah ben Bava, who was lanced to death by the Romans for teaching the Law during the period of religious repression in Palestine that followed the Bar Kokhba revolt.

170   Beitar: A village near Jerusalem, the last bastion of Bar Kokhba's army to fall to the Romans in 135 C.E.

170   Yehudah Halevi: See note to p. 57 on *The Kuzari.*

170   the Baal Or Hayyim: Rabbi Hayyim ben Moses ibn Atar of Morocco (1696–1743), noted cabalist and proponent of Jewish resettlement in Palestine, whose works were widely read in Hasidic circles.

170   the Rabbi of Berditchev: Levi Isaac of Berditchev in the Ukraine (1740–1809), one of the great "first-generation" Hasidic tsaddikim, known especially for his impassioned defenses of the Jewish people before God.

170   the Maggid of Mezritsh: See note to p. 112.

171   Boruch Kossover: An eighteenth-century cabalist whose work did much to popularize the esoteric teachings of the cabala among a wider audience.

171   Levi ben Gerson: See note to p. 57 on *The Wars of the Lord.*

171   *tsimtsum:*   In cabalistic theosophy, the mysteri-

ous contraction of the Godhead into Itself preceding the act of creation.

171 *hitpashtut:* In cabalistic theosophy, the outward expansion of the Godhead into the vacuum formed by the process of *tsimtsum,* the final stage of which involves the creation of the physical universe.

171 Nachmanides: Moses ben Nachman (1195–1270), philosopher and mystic of the Spanish period, an opponent of the rationalist and Aristotelian school of Maimonides. The rabbinical debate that took place over Maimonides' works during the two centuries following his death and that centered around the relation of philosophy to religion constituted one of the great sustained polemics of Jewish history.

171 Abraham Ibn Ezra: Poet and biblical commentator of the Spanish period (1089–1164).

171 David Kimchi: Biblical commentator and grammarian of the Spanish period (1160–1235), and a supporter of Maimonides.

171 the Narboni: Moses of Narbonne (d. 1362), author of a commentary on Maimonides, whose Aristotelian approach he defended.

171 Samuel ben Adret: Rabbi of the Spanish period (1235–1310), a staunch opponent of the philosophy of Maimonides, the teaching of which he sought to ban from Jewish schools.

171 Samuel ben Meir: A son-in-law of Rashi's (see note to p. 167) and talmudic commentator of note (1080–1150).

171 Abraham ben David: Rabbinical authority of southern France (1125–1198), author of a noted critical commentary on Maimonides' *The Strong Hand.*

172 Yedaiah ha-Penini: Philosopher and Hebrew poet of southern France (1270–1340), who vigorously opposed Samuel ben Adret's ban on Maimonides' philosophical works.

172 Joseph Caro: See note to p. 57.

172 Rabbi Azariah of the Adumim: Azariah Rossi of Italy (1511–1578), one of the first medieval rabbis to attempt to study the development of Jewish Law and legend in a historical light. In consequence he brought down on himself the condemnation of his contemporary Joseph Caro, and his writings were banned by a number of rabbinical authorities.

172 Profiat Duran: Philosopher of the Spanish period (1350–1415), and author of a commentary on Maimonides' *Guide to the Perplexed.*

172 Hasdai Crescas: Philosopher of the Spanish period (c. 1340–c. 1410), who criticized the Aristotelian assumptions of Maimonides.

172 Judah Alfachar: Rabbinical authority of the Spanish period (d. 1235). Alfachar attacked Maimonides for attempting to synthesize philosophy and religion, an issue on which he was publicly opposed by David Kimchi.

173 Rabbi Abraham: Abraham ben Maimon (1186–1237), Maimonides' son, who wrote a number of commentaries on his father's works.

173 the world to come: Paradise.

174 the "Hear, O Israel":   See note to p. 102 on the *Shema.*

175 Job and Jeremiah: The Book of Job was permitted to be read on the Ninth of Av because of its subject matter; the Book of Jeremiah, because in rabbinic tradition Jeremiah is considered to have been the author of the Book of Lamentations, the

biblical elegy on the destruction of the First Temple.

175 Mo'ed Katan: A tractate of the Talmud dealing with the laws of mourning.

175 with play wooden swords: To reenact the battles for the Temple fought on the Ninth of Av.

175 the evil lizards: See note to p. 104.

175 phylacteries: The leather thongs bound around the arm and forehead by Orthodox Jews in the course of the morning prayer, in fulfillment of the Mosaic injunction in Deuteronomy 6:8, "And thou shalt bind them for a sign upon thy hand, and they shall be for frontlets between thine eyes."

176 The benches had been turned upside down: A customary symbol of mourning practiced in the synagogue on the Ninth of Av, as are laying the lecterns on the ground, baring the curtain that customarily covers the ark, going barefoot, and wearing ordinary clothes.

176 the melody of the Book of Lamentations: On the eve of the Ninth of Av the Book of Lamentations is read in the synagogue to a special, mournful chant, which is used for the prayer service as well.

177 O wall of the daughter of Zion . . . :   Lamentations 2:18–19, 3:1–10, 21–41.

179 who loveth the stranger, in giving him food and raiment: Deuteronomy 10:18.

182 Thus saith the Lord of hosts . . . :   Zechariah 1:17.

182 Titus: Titus Flavius Vespasianus (40–81), Roman general, and later emperor, who sacked Jerusalem after a lengthy siege in 70 C.E.

184 Every town stands proud on its foundation . . . :

This phrase is from an elegy by the ninth-century Hebrew poet Amitai ben Shefatiah.

187 the Sabbath of Consolation: The first Sabbath after the Ninth of Av, so called because on it the portion read from the Prophets is Isaiah 40, which begins with the verse "Comfort ye, comfort ye, My people."

192 Buckle: Henry Thomas Buckle (1821–1862), British historian, notable for his attempt to put historical writing on a scientific, positivist basis.

192 Spenser: Herbert Spenser (1820–1903), British positivist philosopher.

196 the High Holy Days: See note to p. 146 on the Days of Awe.

199 the *Tsel Olam:* A Hebrew work on popular science ascribed to the sixteenth-century Italian cabalist Matityahu Delacrut.

200 Haskalah books: See Introduction, pp. 8–9.

201 a yeshivah in Lithuania: In the period in question, Lithuania was known throughout Eastern Europe as a center for advanced talmudic studies.

202 Adam Hacohen: Abraham David Hacohen Lebensohn (1789–1878), whose romantic Hebrew poetry was much in vogue during the period of the Haskalah.

202 peas on Passover: Among the few "liberalizing" concessions to the times made by nineteenth-century Orthodox rabbis in Russia was one permitting the poor, who could not afford other food, to eat peas and other legumes on Passover, which had been previously forbidden because of the possibility that they might begin to leaven if kept overlong. Among secularists, "peas on Passover" became a byword for the intransigence of the

Orthodox and their inability to adapt to modern times.

206 A new movement was abroad: See Introduction, pp. 26–28.

208 If I forget thee, O Jerusalem: From Psalms 137:5.

214 I see him, but not now . . . : Numbers 24:17.